Lucky To Say Goodbye

Written by:

William Mowat

CROWN & ANCHOR PUBLISHING

CROWN & ANCHOR PUBLISHING

crownandanchorpublishing@gmail.com

Copyright © 2023, William Mowat, Author
Published in Canada by Crown and Anchor Publishing,
Welland, Ontario L3B 3H9
ISBN 978-1-7380796-0-5

4

Acknowledgement

How lucky am I to have such
Wonderful friends and family
That provide me with
Irreplaceable support and
Inspiration.

Table of Contents

Chapter 1 - The Mountain.. 11

Chapter 2 - The Village.. 21

Chapter 3 - The Gondola 39

Chapter 4 - Town Hall 47

Chapter 5 - Wellness Day 55

Chapter 6 - Roadtrip... 75

Chapter 7 - The Hot Springs.. 99

Chapter 8 - Date Night... 125

Chapter 9 - Aftermath.. 147

Chapter 10 - Lake Louise 153

Chapter 11 - Lake Minnewanka.. 167

Chapter 12 - The Last Supper 193

Chapter 13 - The Return 209

Chapter 14 - The Crossroads... 223

Chapter 15 - New Horizons... 229

8

'How lucky am I to have something that makes saying goodbye so hard.' – A.A. Milne

Chapter 1 - The Mountain

Thomas Hudson and his two daughters took the last few gruelling steps up the rocky bluffs to finally reach the summit of Mount Rundle overlooking the small village of Banff. The summit was cool, as the three stopped in awe of the 1998 summertime Alberta scenery. They looked down upon the village as if it were some far off kingdom. Thom's oldest daughter, Clarabella, or Bella as most people called her, threw her arm around her younger sister, Charlotte.

"Have you ever seen anything like this, Charlotte?" whispered Bella to her sister.

"Four hours and thirty-seven minutes from basecamp to summit. Well done, girls!" proclaimed the proud father.

The girls were exhausted as their faces were flushed red and sweat dripped down their faces. This pinnacle of the mountain made it all worth it. The view gripped their young minds; they had never felt a rush like this or worked so hard to achieve something so gratifying. They were used to classrooms that smelled like mushrooms and violent afternoon teacher breath. Nothing like here, 12,000 feet above sea level. Bella, 18 and Charlotte, 17 had spent most of their days in Toronto, Ontario, where the air was thick, the people were rude, and the landscape was flat.

"I can feel my heartbeat in my shoes," said Charlotte.

"Me too," laughed Bella.

"When I first came to Banff at twenty-one, this is the mountain where I really began to find myself. I must have climbed this mountain twenty times," said Thom proudly.

The girls turned to look at their father, as he looked across the horizon at the endless peaks. They both admired his stoic face as he gazed deep in thought.

"Dad, why did you have to find yourself? What does that mean?" inquired Charlotte.

"Well, around twenty-one or twenty-two years old, you're going to have to start making a lot of decisions and life choices that will affect the rest of your life. You'll start to think about how you want to dedicate yourself and who you want to share your life with. All not easy decisions to make. I left Toronto to come out here and explore, stretch my legs, and use my imagination. I met your mother, and the rest was history," he said as he nonchalantly pointed at both Bella and Charlotte.

"Did you ever climb this mountain with Mom?" asked Bella.

"I sure did. We climbed all sorts of mountains together. We never brought enough water or food with us though. My legs were always seizing up when I was young and ill-prepared. Luckily, I learned my lesson," Thom said as he took a long sip from his canteen.

"Mom would have loved this day," said Bella.

"You bet she would have, kiddo. She's up there right now looking down with a jealous eye," Thom said reassuringly.

"I miss her so much," Charlotte said as she put her head on Bella's shoulder.

All three shared an embrace and sat down on a nearby rock outcrop.

Thom and Valerie met in Banff in 1977 while they were both working summer jobs at a local restaurant on Bear Street. Thom was a cook and Valerie was a waitress. On Thom's first day at work, Val asked him and some others to go out after work, as she was very popular and outgoing with all the staff. Of course, he went along, and Thom still vividly remembers what table they sat at, what she was wearing, and what she ordered to drink. It was the best day of his life.

Banff was a tiny village back then full of thrill seekers, adventurous Europeans and tourists looking to snap some pictures to show people back home. Television wasn't a big deal in Banff, most everyone was about cards, board games and generally, being outdoors. In Thom and Val's first weeks together as a couple, they would play Monopoly, Life and Snakes and Ladders well into the night. They would never run out of things to talk about. It was an interesting time; Star Wars was released, Elvis Presley had died, and the Commodore computer was released. The summer of 1977 was a time that Thom never forgot; the mountains, the air, and that particular point in life when things would never be the same again.

As Thom, Charlotte, and Bella sat on the rocky summit of Mount Rundle, they realized how hard they were breathing. Charlotte had mild asthma growing up and she took out her puffer and took a deep inhale from it.

"I knew a boy from Hamilton, Ontario, who had severe asthma growing up and when he moved here to Banff, he essentially outgrew it. His lungs started working harder, he got super fit and never looked back." As Thom continued the story, both girls seemed to drift from missing their mother to being inquisitive, curious kids again. "His name was Bert. He was one of the prep cooks in our kitchen, and he was hilarious. He was always talking about how the Hamilton Tigercats were a way better team than the

Calgary Stampeders and that they were going to win the Grey Cup. People out here are crazy about the CFL."

"What's the CFL?" asked Charlotte.

"Football, Char, football," Bella answered.

"Bert had this funny little moustache, but it was cool at the time. Most of us were struggling with upper lip hair. I remember this one time, Bert driving a bunch of us out to Canmore to go cliff-jumping. Now, I don't know if you've ever swam in a glacier-fed river before, but trust me, it was freezing. Even in the middle of summer it shocked us to the core."

"Do you think I can beat asthma?" asked Charlotte.

"Definitely," said Thom.

"How high were the cliffs?" asked Bella.

"Probably, around 40 feet," said Thom.

"I could never do that," Charlotte said with a terrified look on her face.

"Mind over matter, Char, mind over matter," Thom said. There was a pause as they continued to rest and soak in the view as the sun was stretching overhead. "Your mother never hesitated. She jumped with so much confidence, girls. When her head popped out of the water, she didn't look so confident. She looked like a blue-lipped ghost," Thom said as they all shared a laugh together.

After the summer of 1977, Thom and Val moved to Guelph, Ontario, leaving the beauty of Banff and the Rockies in the rearview mirror. No more mountains, kitchen board games, or hiking adventures; in came the lectures, late-night studying, and four-hour exams of university life.

Thom enrolled in engineering and Val took physical education at the University of Guelph. They were great, formative years, as they studied and strove towards like-minded, career goals.

Looking back, Thom and Valerie always talked about how those university years went by like a blur.

After they both graduated and got stable jobs, Thom as a clerk at an architecture firm and Val, as a teacher, they were married at a little church in rural countryside outside of the city of Guelph. About 30 people attended their fall wedding. There was freezing rain the night before, so everything was coated in ice but appeared to be smooth glass. The wedding pictures had a magical quality that many people complimented; the blades of frozen grass and the reflections on the fence that lined the church property.

As Val found work within Guelph, they naturally bought a house within city limits. It was a modest three-bedroom house tucked in behind a small bush of pine and white cedars. Val always loved the smell of home and the privacy the evergreens provided.

Thom, on the other hand, commuted to Toronto, which was an hour away from home. Though it was far, he loved the drive, as it prepared him for the rigours of daily work and allowed him to decompress before he got home. He loved getting home. Val was always home before he was and cooking something delicious, building something, or rigorously marking student's work. Thom was always eager to see what Val was doing. Sometimes she had done something in the garden, or painted a room, or done some other unique craft. Thom loved her creativity, her energy, and her talent for getting things done.

In the first year of marriage, Bella was born and the year after, Charlotte came into the world. Both girls grew up in the Guelph house until they moved to Toronto in 1988. Val had taken a ministry job with the Ontario government which meant that both parents needed to be close to Toronto. The girls always despised their move to the big city; moving away from their friends and comfort zone into the hustling, bustling city where they were forced to take, often filthy subways and breathe the thick city air.

The girls did eventually get used to things in Toronto. School seemed to get better, and the air seemed easier to breathe. They found new movie theatres, concert venues, parks, museums, and all sorts of cuisines throughout the city. They loved the Greek food on the Danforth, the cafés in Little Italy and certainly all the new sushi restaurants that were popping up along Bloor Street.

By the mid-nineties, the girls loved playing volleyball and baseball, they loved Grunge music, Nirvana, Soundgarden and anything to do with Wynona Ryder or River Phoenix. It was the fondest time in Thom's life. The girls were flourishing and becoming individuals, his wife was on top in her career, and Thom was a senior manager at his design firm.

Then, in 1995, Valerie developed a horrible fever. Doctors ultimately discovered cancer in the tissues of her gallbladder. She fought hard for two years until she eventually passed away peacefully at Toronto General Hospital in the winter of 1997. Bella had just turned 16 and Charlotte was 15 at the time.

For the months following their mother's death, Thom and the girls struggled. For Thom, everything was a blur. He had trouble eating, sleeping, and focusing on anything. He initially felt guilty thinking it may have been his fault and then shifted to the guilt of feeling it should have been him that died and not Valerie. The first months were an incredible struggle for everyone.

Bella and Charlotte had difficulty making any type of decision and, like Thom, they lost their interest in eating, they both failed classes, isolated themselves, and generally lost interest in their friends, hobbies, and work. Clearly, they were devastated by their mother's loss.

The grieving process was affecting them all differently. Thom hired a therapist for them to see twice a week to help cope with the loss of their caring and devoted mother. The therapist guided them through incredible lessons about open and honest communication, adjusting to a new life, eating properly, sleeping well, exercise, and not making any major life decisions during the grieving period.

A few months into the sessions, the therapist suggested creating some new memories and visiting places of interest outside of their typical days and routines. Bella and Charlotte went to Ottawa to visit their grandparents, they went to Quebec City for a week and journeyed to Niagara Falls for a weekend. The process was beginning to work.

Thom began to acknowledge the importance of eating and sleeping properly. He got all his financial affairs in order, he wrote a new will, he consulted with a new attorney, he shifted everything into his name and began to be aware of his new responsibility for both himself and his daughters. Eventually he went through Valerie's belongings; he donated some things, sold some things, and kept a few sentimental items that he treasured. After the first year, he was moving at his own pace again.

The girls were on the mend, as well. They found their support systems, including each other. They regained their appetite, their sleep habits changed, and they re-engaged in school. Thom was super proud of his girls and himself as they all avoided any serious, complicated grief. They overcame their loss with incredible support from the community, their family, professionals and, most of all, each other.

Thom had waited until the right moment with Charlotte and Bella to finally share what he had been holding back for days. "Girls, I've got some news for you," he said.

"Good or bad?" Bella inquired.

"I guess it depends. I've just put in an offer on a house in Caledon, a little town north of the city. It is a cute little rural property, fairly close to where you grew up. Just waiting to seal the deal," Thom said as both girls were at a loss for words.

"Are you selling the Toronto house?" asked Charlotte.

"I think so. Bella's off to university, and you'll be off next year," Thom replied.

"So, I have to spend my final year at a different high school?" Charlotte cried.

"No, I'm going to drive you to school and pick you up every day, and if you need to stay over somewhere, you can stay with Keagan at the Willoughby's place."

"That's not fair. Do you have any idea what it's like to get dropped off by your parents? Can you just buy me a car?" asked Charlotte.

"That's actually a pretty good idea, Char. We'll see if it's in the finances; we'll talk about it," said Thom. They all shared a pause. "I think we need to move out of that house. You both will love Caledon. The house I am looking at is much bigger and I bet you're both going to love it. It reminds me of our old home. Beautiful property with cedar trees and a long driveway. I wanted to tell you when we were out here and surprise you. Both of you, your mother, and I spent a lot of time in that old house in Toronto and I think it's time for us to move on."

There was another pause as the wind picked up around them. The pines deep in the valley began to sway harder and dust began to swirl at the summit and along the dragon's back of the mountain where the three were observing.

"I miss her so much," Charlotte cried as she threw her head on her dad's shoulder.

"I know, sweetness. I miss her too." Thom placed his head atop Charlotte's.

"I think it's a good move, Dad, selling the house, I mean. There's a lot of great memories there, but it's about moving forward, right?" Bella said in a mature tone.

"Thanks, Bella. This last year and a half has been hard on all of us. You're going to university, you're going to go on amazing adventures and meet new, exciting people in your life. Things are going to get so much better," Thom explained.

"Maybe you'll meet somebody else," Charlotte said to her father.

"Ha. Maybe, Char, maybe. Do you guys want to get off this mountain? It looks like the winds are picking up and I definitely want to be off by sundown," he said, noticing the sun starting to set.

"Yeah, let's get out of here," said Charlotte getting up.

"But let's get a picture first, I want to remember this moment forever," Bella exclaimed.

The three of them got together, shoulder to shoulder and took a few pictures with a Pentax camera Bella had with her. The sun shone on their rosy cheeks as wind blew their hair everywhere. It was a great climb; a day certainly to remember. After they finished taking a few pictures, the three of them descended back down the rough terrain into the village of Banff.

Chapter 2 - The Village

The small village of Banff was an energetic one. There were souvenir shops, restaurants, bakeries, ski and snowboard shops, hostels, hotels, and cafés everywhere. People dotted the streets with bright and fluorescent-coloured clothes and various shopping bags. Thom was sort of familiar with the Banff culture, however it was all new to Bella and Charlotte.

The lodge where Thom, Bella, and Charlotte were staying was grandiose, complete with 30-foot ceilings, stone-hearth fireplaces, taxidermy along the walls, and people from all over the world. Germans, Swiss, Americans, Australians, and Czechs sat in various spots throughout the lounge area, where several different accents could be heard above the radio in the background. Everyone was very fit, as clearly, they were here to hike and not just shop. The three made their way past the lobby and up the lodge stairs to their room.

Their room had a small kitchen and living space, two bedrooms and a bathroom. The three immediately collapsed from exhaustion. Without saying a word, the three dropped all their heavy gear, peeled off a few sweaty layers of clothes, and tore off their shoes. All three of them groaned with relief after the gruelling day-long hike.

"Let's meet down in the restaurant in an hour for some dinner. I saw they're serving ribeye steaks tonight. Sound good girls?" asked Thom as Charlotte and Bella groaned their affirmation. "Great, I'm going to head out, there's a few things I want to grab before tomorrow's adventure."

"Ok, Dad. Be safe," Bella said.

Thom grabbed a light jacket and went back out to where they had just come from. Bella looked confused, while Charlotte just looked dead.

"What is his problem?" asked Bella.

"He has too much energy," replied Charlotte.

"No kidding. Seems like he's right at home," Bella said as she dropped on the couch. "My legs are jelly."

"So, what do you think about dad selling the house?" asked Charlotte.

"The house is hard to live in right now. Every corner of that house has a memory which I don't like to recall every time I see it. Sitting on the kitchen island with mom making cookies, mom putting band-aids on our scratches, feeding the birds on the back porch; every time I turn my head, I end up being reminded of her and it tears me up," Bella said thoughtfully and emotionally.

"Yeah, but isn't that a good thing? I like thinking about her. She loved us, Bella. She comforted us when we were down, she made us feel better, and she made sure all of us knew we were loved," Charlotte responded.

"I know, Charlotte, but trust me, it will be much easier to heal without constant salt in the wounds. Mom would want us to heal and move on, especially since it was so sudden and so difficult for everyone, Dad especially," said Bella.

The two girls were obviously exhausted and could hardly keep their eyes open. Bella stood up with a moan: "I'm going to shower."

As Bella went into the bathroom, Charlotte was thinking heavily. She was always the baby of the family, but now she was being asked to grow up very quickly. Her mother was no longer in her life, she was going to start driving, picking universities, grocery shopping, paying taxes, it was too much, too soon. She started to cry a little as she reflected on how her Mom and Dad met within the village of Banff. She couldn't help the feelings that were engulfing her.

Charlotte never had a serious boyfriend, but in times like this, she sure wished she had one. Someone to make her laugh and forget about all the angst of the time. She wanted someone to take her to the movies and get ice cream. She wanted someone to listen to music with and go on adventures with. Though she was with Bella and her dad, she felt painfully alone.

While Bella was in the shower, Charlotte went to the balcony which overlooked the railway tracks that ran alongside the town. In the far distance, a herd of elk could be seen as they grazed the summer grass. It was amazing how such wild creatures were grazing next to traffic and so close to town, she thought. Banff truly was a magical place as she looked up on Cascade Mountain, the biggest mountain for miles around. Though it had only been a day, this place truly felt magical. She wondered if her mom ever looked out to the mountains, as she was, with the same awe, emotion, and joy.

Knowing only Ontario for her whole life, this place seemed to immediately open up Charlotte's perspective on the vastness of Canada. She always thought Canada was a small world, full of streetcars, automobiles, chain stores, and gas stations. Seeing the cascading landscapes was a reminder that her story was just beginning and not at the end.

Bella screamed from inside the room, "Showers free!"

"Ok, thanks!" Charlotte turned to go inside, but pivoted to get a last glimpse of the mountains and ingrain it as a moment she would remember forever.

Thom walked down Banff Avenue, the main street in town, with only two goals in mind: one, to find his girls a cute little memento of the day and two, to find a rarified, spectacular coffee that would keep his eyes open for the next 2-4 hours as he battled exhaustion and jet lag.

Thom loved walking here; memories came flooding back with each passing block. All the fresh air and mountain backdrop made for a joyous promenade. It was nothing like walking in Toronto, where everyone seemed to be in a rush, or they were asking for something, or it was smoggy, busy, noisy, or depressing. The only time Thom enjoyed walking in Toronto was at nighttime, so he didn't have to share the sidewalk with 4x4 posses and double-wide strollers.

Everything in the town reminded Thomas of Valerie; the walks they shared, the pancake breakfasts, buying stamps, shopping at tourist traps, and everything else along the village streets. Thom popped into a gift store that had all the typical Banff tourist stuff; shot glasses, cheap t-shirts, stuffed moose, and toy beavers. Thom wanted to find something thoughtful and reflective; a key chain wasn't going to cut it.

As he exited the store empty-handed, he saw a coffee shop across the street. It was a cute little operation with a moderate little sign that read 'The Bean'. Outside the plate glass windows, there were a couple benches and a chalkboard with the daily specials. Inside he could see it was open and was serving just what he was looking for: fresh coffee.

As he crossed the street, he began to smell the beautiful aroma and it lit up his endorphins. Thom was used to waiting in long Toronto line-ups for terrible, overpriced coffee, where they showed zero gratitude for him or his business. He knew, after such a long day-hike, this might be the best coffee he ever tasted.

Thom entered the coffee shop with a cool confidence. His legs were burning, but it was the type of pain he welcomed. To his right, he saw a group of young cool kids, decked out in all the hip swag of the late 1990s; Quiksilver t-shirts, Solomon hiking boots, and cargo shorts straight off the cover of a Pearl Jam album cover. He played it cool and sent a little smile their way. To his left, there was a smart looking woman sipping a cappuccino with a couple of books and a set of blueprints in front of her. Her casual dress suggested she may have been a local working in the area. She certainly didn't look like one of those stand-out Swedish tourists with excess fluorescent clothing and bleach blonde hair.

Thom was immediately interested in the woman. Not only was she pretty, but she also had blueprints in front of her, which was right up his alley. He ordered a large black coffee from the indifferent teenager, who seemed to rather be anywhere but here serving his coffee. After ordering, he leaned on the counter so he could peer at what the mysterious woman was doing and what the blueprints were outlining.

Thom got his coffee and smelled it with great anticipation. He slowly walked over to the lady at the table. "Hi there, sorry to interrupt, but I couldn't help but notice the blueprints. I'm an architect and engineer visiting from Ontario. Blueprints kind of get me excited."

"Oh, do they?" the lady giggled.

"Not that kind of excited," Thom smiled. "It's just nice to see some like-minded people here amongst the righteous and gnarly," he said nodding to the group of cool kids behind him.

"What's your expertise?" she inquired.

"I'm mostly into designing commercial architecture in Toronto and the G.T.A. I'm Thom by the way."

"I'm Lacy."

"Nice to meet you, Lacy."

The two shared a nice pause. This is the first woman that Thom struck up a conversation with in over two years. He was reminded of the energy of a woman and how it made him want to become a better person. Lacy's smile and laid-back confidence was somehow soothing the stress that had accumulated over the past couple of years.

"I'm a parking and traffic engineer for Banff. Maybe not as lucrative or fancy as your commercial licence," Lacy said.

"That's amazing. My job is mostly designing box stores and making sure they have proper connections to all the amenities. I work for a pretty big firm with lots of great contracts, but they have a knack for burying talent, if you catch my drift," Thom said.

"Completely. It sounds like most firms, where talent is more of a threat than an opportunity," Lacy said thoughtfully.

"Exactly. Walking on eggshells wherever you go. So, do you live in Banff?" asked Thom.

"I've been here for five years now. I've done a lot of work with Fairmont and Banff Springs, most of the hotels and parks. It's a great gig." Lacy smiled at Thom, as he peered at the blueprints of what was seemingly a hotel with a parking lot adjacent to a road.

"Seems like you'd have a lot of interesting projects," Thom said.

"Definitely. No two projects are the same," Lacy answered.

"I know this seems pretty forward, but do you, by chance, have dinner plans?" Thom boldly asked.

"I do, I'm sorry. I'm meeting some colleagues at Earl's." Lacy said with a frown.

"Sorry, I didn't mean to impose." Thom's face flushed red.

"Don't be sorry. There's a bunch of us going for drinks after, maybe you could pop by St. James Gate at around 9:00pm?" Lacy said with a smile.

"St. James Gate around 9:00pm? That sounds great," Thom said.

"Do you know where it is?"

"Yeah, I know exactly where it is," Thom answered with a smile. "I'm staying over at the Moose Lodge and meeting my daughters, so I've gotta fly. So great meeting you, Lacy." Thom turned to the door. "I'm looking forward to seeing you later on."

"Bye, Thom," Lacy said as she turned to her blueprints smiling and shaking her head.

Thom exited the coffee shop with a stupid looking grin on his face. He took a big gulp from his coffee and started walking the street. As he strolled, he had a euphoric feeling about him. He felt the best he had since he first met Valerie all those years ago. He felt incredible happiness and pride in himself; it had been so long since he took a leap of faith and was rewarded for his efforts.

He also remembered his initial reason for his journey; he wanted to buy Bella and Charlotte a small gift. As he was thinking about what he could possibly get, Thom saw an Indigenous woman on the other side of the street weaving something with thread and needle. He couldn't quite make it out, but he was curious. He looked both ways and crossed the street. As he got closer, he realized she was weaving beautiful dream catchers. Thom wasn't quite sure what the purpose was, but he wanted to know. As he approached, the woman kept focused on the task of weaving, paying no attention to the newcomer.

"Hi there," Thom said lightly.

"Hello," she replied. "The purpose of the asabikeshiinh or the dream catcher is to protect your children from evil spirits and nightmares. It is woven like a spider's web to catch all the bad spirits," she said, while still looking down.

Thom noticed she had several dream catchers at her feet. "This is amazing work. My children have been having a hard time lately and this might help the bad dreams and terrible thoughts."

"What disturbs them? Who have they lost?" asked the Indigenous woman.

"Their mother. How did you know?" Thom was shocked by her intuition. He sat down beside her on the ledge of a flower bed.

"The night air is filled with dreams. The dream catcher hangs over the beds and protects them as the nightmares hover." The woman finally looked up to Thom. "An old woman noticed a spider weaving a web above her bed. Her boy went to kill the spider and the old woman stopped him. The spider was thankful and promised to protect her children from nightmares. The hoop represents the circle of life. The beads represent the spider and the feathers represent a soft path for good dreams to follow."

"Thank you. My girls need protection. It has been a terrible path they've been on. Their mother passed on. I'm terribly worried about them," Thom said as he looked down at his shoes.

"Take these." She handed him two dreamcatchers about six inches wide.

"I pray these will work," Thom said thankfully. "How much do you charge for them?"

"Anything you may offer," she said.

"Here's a hundred. This means a lot. It's very special and I thank you for your kindness and wisdom," Thom said gratefully.

"Thank you for your kindness. Your daughters will welcome their dreams and the spider that will protect them. Thank you for a good trade."

"A good trade indeed. Thank you." Thom rose to his feet.

"Thank you," she said as she looked back down to her craft.

As Thom walked back towards the lodge, he admired the beauty and detail the woman put into the dream catchers, beautiful oceanic and crimson colours with striking feathers and sparkling beads.

The sun was now behind the mountains, as he walked and finished his coffee. His stomach was rumbling, and he was excited to see the girls and give them their gift of good dreams and protection against nightmares.

The girls were sitting at a large, hand-crafted wooden table set with silverware and water glasses. The dining room had a warm glow with a large elk head hanging over the large mantle on a stone fireplace. The aroma of rosemary and garlic butter filled the air as the girls looked through different brochures they had picked up in the lobby.

Thom entered the dining room and saw his two girls at the table patiently waiting for their father. He paused, took a deep breath, and admired the composure and grace of Bella and Charlotte in such a warm, cozy environment.

"Hi Dad!" said Charlotte.

"Hiya kiddos."

"What do you have there?" asked Bella.

"It's a small little present I picked up. They're dream catchers. One for each of you."

"So pretty," said Charlotte.

"I got them from a lady hand-making them on Banff Avenue. They're meant to protect you from nightmares. They represent a spider and her web that traps the bad dreams and allows the good dreams to pass," Thom explained.

"So neat," Bella said. "Thanks, dad."

"Yeah, thanks dad. They're so pretty. Can we order? I'm starving!" Charlotte said, quickly changing the subject.

"Yes! I'm starving. Let's eat!" Thom shouted.

Lacy arrived at St. James Gate pub around 8:00pm after dinner with a group of colleagues. The pub was in the Old English style, with brass taps, dart boards, low ceilings, and complete with green upholstery and red carpets. St. James Gate wasn't a tourist attraction, it was more of a place where locals hang out; restaurant industry people looking to unwind after long shifts.

The pub was packed with characters; old men with various styles of facial hair sat at the bar with their Guinness pints. Industry people crowded the booths with dozens of empty shot glasses and squeezed lemons. A lone older woman was reading a novel and drinking red wine and there were some loud snowboarders playing darts near the back of the pub. The place was loud, but you could still hear the person next to you.

Lacy, two city hall secretaries, Barb and Tammy, grabbed a table near the centre of the room, while Rob, Jeff, and Pete grabbed drinks at the bar.

"Six pints of Newcastle!" Rob yelled to the bartender.

The bartender cocked his head so he could hear better.

"Six pints of Newcastle!" he yelled again.

"Gotcha!" the bartender responded.

Jeff, Rob, and Pete brought the beers back to the table where Lacy, Tammy, and Barb were sitting. All the friends were in their mid to late thirties and had been close for years. The St. James Pub was one of their favourite places in town and was a weekly tradition. The colleagues would often celebrate special occasions, grab dinner, have some drinks, or come to socialize at the fun, popular pub.

The snowboarders were constantly yelling and giving each other high fives. Clearly, the lagers were getting to them, but everyone ignored the ruckus because they knew they weren't hurting anyone. Banff was full of drifters and adrenaline junkies.

Most of them worked at restaurants, hit the slopes in their off time and drank like fish at night: it was a lifestyle.

The lady in the corner who was reading, sipped her red wine every couple of minutes, occasionally looking up to judge the rest of the people in the bar. Nobody could understand how she was able to read among the noise and carnage of the environment, but nonetheless, she endured.

An old man got up from the bar every few minutes and made his way to the washroom. You could almost synchronise your watch to which old man would go to the washroom next. Nobody knew what these old men did in town, but they were the healthiest looking old men you would ever see. They were thin, calm, cool and intelligent looking, despite the odd stumble on the way to the can.

Lacy and her colleagues all raised their glasses and shared cheers together.

"Another great week together," said Rob.

"Here's to the long straight piece in Tetris," said Pete.

All shared a laugh.

"Why do you think that lady reads in here with all this noise?" Barb asked.

"I think it's because she's looking for a man and wants to come across as intelligent and refined," Tammy said. "It's kind of cute."

"It's kind of sad," Jeff frowned.

"Let's hook her up with one of the old guys at the bar," Rob suggested. "Watch this."

Rob stood up with his drink and walked over to the old men at the bar and began speaking to them. Tammy, Lacy, Barb, Jeff, and Pete couldn't make out what they were talking about, but they noticed how intently they were listening to Rob's words.

As they were all staring at the bar, an old man stood up and turned towards the lady with a ridiculous prideful look. He straightened up, held his chin up high and walked towards the mysterious woman in the corner. Everyone watched intently as the drama was about to unfold.

The bearded man arrived at the table and the two shared a few words. The lady smiled at him and indicated for him to sit down. The old man sat down and the two became engaged in conversation.

The five friends stared in shock and awe. They all then looked at Rob at the bar where he and the rest of the old men were smiling with glee and pride. Rob picked up his beer and returned to the table with a small tray of six shots of tequila, complete with six wedges of lemon. The friends watched every step as Rob returned to his colleagues at the table with a huge smile on his face.

"What just happened?!" asked Tammy impatiently.

"Just a little matchmaking," Rob replied.

"Amazing," Pete said as he leaned back in his chair, shocked.

"I just told him what the book she was reading was about. Hopefully he doesn't have to keep it up for long," Rob said in a proud voice.

Charlotte and Bella were in their pyjamas lounging in their room watching The Parent Trap on T.V. Both girls were clearly exhausted from the long day and the big meal they just had.

"Lindsay Lohan is so cute. She's got a bright future," Bella observed.

"Does she actually have a twin sister?" Charlotte innocently asked.

"No dummy. It's special effects," Bella said, rolling her eyes.

"You're a dummy," rebuked Charlotte, clearly exhausted. "Where did Dad say he was going?"

"He said he was going for a walk to clear his head," Bella explained.

"Can we watch something else?" asked Charlotte.

"The only other movie is Batman and Robin or it's the Calgary news."

Charlotte quickly changed the conversation. "Do you think Dad will ever find somebody else?"

Bella looked at her with deep concern. "I doubt it. Mom meant the world to him. He'll probably never be able to look at another woman."

Charlotte looked happy with her response. "Good, I don't think I can deal with a stepparent. Is it true that all stepparents hate their stepchildren?"

"Yes. There's a verse in the Bible outlying that all stepchildren should be treated like filthy dogs. They should be smacked, looked down upon, and fed outside," Bella joked as she giggled at herself and the movie.

Bella looked over at Charlotte and saw she was asleep with her mouth wide open. "Don't worry, Charlotte, Dad doesn't have it in him to meet another woman." Bella rolled over with a smile and slowly dozed off into slumberland.

Thom walked down the street feeling a bulge in his stomach that was the result of a 16-ounce ribeye steak, green beans, and a baked potato. He was tired. It was a long day of climbing a mountain for the first time in many years. His legs were jelly, and his heart was pounding in anticipation of Lacy and her friends at the pub.

It was a clear night and stars were brighter than anywhere or anytime near Toronto. He forgot about the stars and the metaphysical contemplations he would have when they were out. It's almost as if the stars didn't exist in Toronto; smog, light pollution, constant traffic, and people stalking the sidewalks as they rushed toward, whatever, totally ignoring their place in the universe.

People smiled as they passed here. The air was pure. He felt better here. Before he knew it, Thom arrived at the St. James Gate Pub. He looked in through the window and saw it was packed. He noticed the old men at the bar, the snowboarders playing darts, and the new acquaintances in the corner sharing a bottle of red wine. Thom took a deep breath and went inside.

Lacy saw Thom come in through the big brass door and immediately looked back to her friends in order to act surprised when he approached the table. Lacy didn't tell her friends that Thom was going to meet her there, in case he didn't show up and she looked like she was stood-up.

Thom looked and felt good. He wore a nice shirt, pants, and light jacket. He approached the bar, looked around but couldn't find Lacy, so he sat at a stool and ordered a beer. When it arrived on the coaster in front of him, he couldn't help but think of how extroverted he was on this day. For the past two years he hardly talked to anyone, yet alone going out of his way to talk to a girl. His friends and colleagues in Toronto would ask Thom to go out but he always had an excuse; lots of work, daughter things, appointments, etc. This vacation had already proven there was a large piece of him that had been missing. The frosty English pale ale was a symbol of new beginnings.

Thom took a big sip of his beer and licked the frothy stache off his upper lip. He then casually spun his bar stool to take a look at the crowd. He saw Lacy with a group of friends who seemed to be enjoying themselves, as there were empty shot and pint glasses scattered throughout their table.

This is it, he thought. He grabbed his beer and made his way towards Lacy's table. He couldn't help but to think of 'Gimme

Shelter' by The Rolling Stones, like he was Henry Hill walking in slow motion toward the table. Everything was vivid and clear, the colours of the bar, the smell of the chicken wings, and the energy of all the pub goers.

When he arrived at the table, everyone looked up at Thom, except Lacy and Tammy who were exchanging conversation. "Hi there," Thom said faintly. Lacy looked up and smiled.

"Hi, Thom," said Lacy joyfully. She rose out of her seat. "I'm glad you could stop by." She gave him a little, half-hearted hug and they both sat down.

"This place is great," Thom said, as he looked around at the group and began shaking the hands of Tammy, Barb, Jeff, Rob, and Pete. "Hi, I'm Thom."

"Hi, Thom," said Barb seductively.

"I met Thom at the Bean today. He's an architect from Ontario," Lacy said. "He noticed my drawings and made the connection."

"Always great to meet a fellow engineer," Rob said.

"What brings you to Banff?" Pete asked.

"Well, me and my two daughters are on summer vacation. So, it's nice to talk about something besides The Backstreet Boys and Alanis Morrisette," Thom explained.

Everyone shared a laugh. Tammy and Barb began singing 'Ironic' by Alanis Morrisette. Soon the rest joined in.

> *It's like rain on your wedding day.*
> *It's a free ride when you've already paid.*
> *It's the good advice that you just didn't take.*
> *And who would've thought? It figures.*

Lacy looked at Thom as everyone was singing. He was laughing and enjoying the moment.

"Barb, Lacy, let's go to the jukebox!" Tammy said as she rose from her seat.

The three women went to the jukebox as Thom took a seat with Rob, Jeff, and Pete. The energy of these newfound friends felt like being a kid again. An energy that was sorely missed and needed in his life. "So, do all of you work together?" Thom asked.

"I do most of the work," Pete immediately chimed in. "These guys do most of the loafing and slacking."

"We're all at townhall. Pete's in finance. Rob's in public and media relations and I'm in facilities administration," Jeff explained.

"That's terrific," Thom said as he thought how nice it was to be surrounded by professionals that still knew how to have a good time.

"So, how long are you here for, Thom?" asked Rob.

"Two weeks total. My girls and I hiked Mount Rundle today. What a blast."

"Great day for a hike. How was it at 2000 metres above sea level?" Jeff asked.

"Pretty brisk, but the sun kept us warm. Took us about 8 hours. It was the first mountain climbing experience for the girls, so we took our time," Thom explained. "We are thinking about climbing Sulphur Mountain next and taking the gondola back down."

Eventually the girls returned to the table smiling and the song 'As Long as You Love Me' by The Backstreet Boys came on the jukebox. Thom rolled his eyes. One of the snowboarders playing darts yelled: "I hate this song with a fiery passion!" Everyone shared a laugh as Tammy, Barb, and Lacy seemed unphased as they were singing along with the jukebox.

As the night went on, Thom had a few beers but kept himself under control. His six new friends on the other hand, were carrying on a Friday night tradition of celebrating another hard week done. Thom didn't mind. This was a great night. They talked about Toronto, the 401, Mike Harris, Bill Clinton, Princess Diana, and a new thing called Google. They played darts, sang songs, and played everything in the jukebox, from Dianna Ross to Pearl Jam.

At the end of the night, Thom, Lacy, Barb, Tammy, Jeff, Rob, and Pete all left St. James Gate Pub together and gathered on the sidewalk. Nobody really drove in Banff, so no one had to worry about anyone driving anywhere.

"So where are you staying, Thom?" asked Tammy.

"Over at the Moose Lodge," Thom responded.

"We are all going to see a movie on Wednesday night, if you want to come," Lacy suggested.

"What movie?" Thom responded.

Lacy looked surprised. "Does it matter which movie?" she said laughing.

"Of course, it does," Thom said with a straight face, then burst into laughter.

Everyone giggled. "Titanic is showing, but Deep Impact is opening, so I think we are going to see that. The theatre is right across the street there," Jeff said while pointing. "We usually meet at the Saltlik around 6:00pm for a pre-movie bite to eat."

"That sounds terrific. Man, I'm so glad that I've met you folks. I've had such a blast," Thom said genuinely. "I can't wait until Wednesday to do some more adulting." He smiled at everyone but held his gaze a little longer on Lacy who was smiling back at him.

"Bye Thom, see you Wednesday night," Lacy said.

"See you soon!" Thom turned and began walking back toward the lodge as the others went in the opposite direction.

He couldn't help but think of sleep as his exhaustion was making him feel twice as drunk as he was. When he arrived at his room, he was extra quiet, he didn't want his girls knowing he was drinking until last call. He took off his shoes, his jacket, shirt, and while taking off his pants, he took an awkward spill into the nightstand knocking off the lamp causing a huge racket. "Crap, balls!"

He paused and realized his clumsy manoeuvre didn't wake up the girls. He just laid there silent on the floor with his pants around his ankles. Looking at the ceiling, he laughed to himself. He finally got up and made his way to the bed and fell asleep within 30 seconds of hitting the pillow.

Chapter 3 - The Gondola

Bella was the first to wake. As she opened her eyes she was slightly confused as to where she was. She eventually remembered as she looked at Charlotte sleeping next to her with her mouth still wide open. Charlotte snored like a 70-year-old man. As she stretched, she felt the pain throughout her body, but it was a good pain, the type she openly welcomed. She didn't want to move at all; she was convinced she slept in the exact same position throughout the night and hadn't moved an inch.

Bella sat up, threw on some clothes, and made her way down to the dining room to get a bite to eat. She rarely woke up hungry, but today was different. It was one of the first things she thought about. There was a small little buffet set up with fresh fruit, scrambled eggs, bacon, and bagels spread about. Perfect, she thought. She loaded up a huge plate with everything and sat down at a table and began eating.

The food tasted great. As she poured ketchup on her plate, she started to recall the hike up Mount Rundle the day before, the trees, the switchbacks, the dragon's back, and the summit of the giant mountain. She also began thinking about starting university in September and what post-secondary life was going to be like. She still had no idea which school she was going to choose. She wanted to tour each campus before she decided. She knew she would have to move into a strange residence on her own, she would have to cook her own meals, organize her own schedule, and become her own boss. Though she would miss being the big fish in the little pond, she was looking forward to the mature life of a post-secondary student.

Bella's final two years of high school were mostly just the arduous strain of academics. She visited her mother at the hospital almost every day during those sad times and was barely able to complete her courses. She recalls the chemotherapy, the nurses, the smells, the uncomfortable chairs, and the constant fluorescent light of the hospital. Though some teenagers would welcome the waves of attention that stem from a loved one dying, she hated the constant comforting and sympathy from her teachers and peers. Her friends understood it was difficult and important to take her mind away from her dying mother, but others who constantly brought it up just reminded her of the pain. In certain times she would blame others for the pain she was in; often she would end up in the principal's office for lashing out on her classmates.

Bella always felt the most pain in the moments her mother would have loved; her high school graduation, her acceptance into university, and moments like yesterday as she and her sister climbed their first mountain. She also thought about times in the future that might upset her; her first job, her engagement, her wedding, her first born child, and times when her mom's eyes would have welled-up with tears of pride.

Bella was thankful she was old enough to understand what was happening with her mother and relatively mature enough to cope with it. Charlotte always took their mother's passing worse than she did, but Bella understood that everyone grieves differently. Charlotte cried a lot, her grades fell almost completely off, she complained and sulked more, became hyper-defensive and lost interest in playing her favourite sports; baseball, and volleyball. Bella felt terrible for her sister, but knew she was just a little lost and needed to find her way back to the path with all the proper support.

Bella munched her entire plate. Just as she finished her last bite, a young handsome busboy came along and asked if she was finished with her plate. She said 'yes' and smiled while looking up at the young man. There was an immediate connection between the two young adults.

"How are you enjoying your stay so far?" he boldly asked.

"This is my first time in Banff, actually it's my first time in the Rocky Mountains," Bella said blushing.

"I saw you, your dad and sister in here last night for supper."

"Yeah, we're on summer vacation for a couple weeks. The food here is amazing, by the way," Bella said earnestly.

"My folks run the lodge. My dad is the head chef, and my mom does all the administration stuff. I'm Brody, by the way. It's nice to meet you," he said, extending his hand.

Bella shook his hand with pleasure. He was tall, mysterious, and clearly a hard worker. Just as they were exchanging their handshake, Charlotte and Thom came into the dining room.

"Hi, Bella!" yelled Charlotte.

"So, your name is Bella?" Brody asked.

"It's Clarabella, but everyone calls me Bella," she said to Brody. "This is Charlotte and my dad, Mr. Thomas Hudson."

"Hi there, young man. How's the coffee? I need a jump-start this morning," Thom said using his dad-humour voice.

"Sure thing, Mr. Hudson, I'll be right back. Anything for you, Charlotte?" asked Brody.

"Is there orange juice here?" Charlotte asked.

"Sure is. I'll be right back with coffee and O.J.," Brody said in his best professional voice. "Help yourself to the buffet whenever you're ready."

As soon as Brody was gone, Charlotte couldn't help herself. "Oh vey! Bella's got a boyfriend! Bella's got a boyfriend!"

"Charlotte, behave yourself. What a nice young man," said Thom as he rubbed his temple, clearly feeling a little pain from the night before.

"His name is Brody," Bella said. "His parents own the lodge."

"Is he single?" Charlotte asked provocatively.

"You shut your mouth," Bella said in a threatening tone.

"Girls, relax," Thom intervened. "It's way too early for fist fights. Let's eat some breakfast and head out soon. It looks like it's going to be a beautiful day."

Thom, Charlotte, and Bella ate a big breakfast and went back to their rooms to gather their things for the hike up Sulphur Mountain. Banff was bustling at 9:00am when they left. The streets were full of adventurous looking people; trendy people, people with either hiking boots or Birkenstocks, people wearing custom hemp necklaces, and people sporting three-hundred-dollar backpacks from Mountain Equipment Co-op. This town didn't put their careers first, they put their recreation before all else.

It did not take long for Bella and Charlotte to feel right at home in this small town. High energy, good food, and no traffic made for a less stressful and less anxious place. Toronto was busy, fast-paced, and had limited green space. Both felt healthier only after a day; their eyes seemed stronger, their muscles seemed tighter, and their souls felt uplifted. They had been on vacation before; they'd been camping, been to Europe, tanned on exotic beaches, but never where there were incredible mountains with rewarding views.

The base of Sulphur Mountain was in the morning shadows, so the beginning of the hike was cool and refreshing. Sulphur was probably the most popular mountain in Banff due to the world-famous gondola and its relative proximity to the Banff Springs Hotel.

Thom and the girls began the six-hour hike with sore legs but warmed up as they began the first few hundred metres. Switch-back after switch-back, the view seemed to change every time. They would find themselves underneath the gondola as cars passed overhead. The next out-cropping would be staring down at the Fairmont Banff Springs Hotel. It was a rewarding hike. Their legs started to burn as they made their way to the top of the mountain.

Once Thom, Bella, and Charlotte made it to the top of the mountain, they followed a boardwalk along the south ridge to a large pavilion, complete with a small museum, washrooms, and a gift shop. The three were exhausted, though it was only half the hike from yesterday. The three sat at a handmade wood bench overlooking the Village of Banff. They had some snacks and drank some water while they rested.

"Quite a view, isn't it," Thom said. "Me and your mom would climb this sucker about once a week, then we would go to the hot springs below."

"Hot springs?" Charlotte asked.

"There are a couple of them down on the other side of Sulphur. Maybe we'll go tomorrow."

"What is it?" Charlotte again inquired.

"Well, it's a geological phenomenon that heats a body of water through geothermal energy. It heats the mantle and cools as it makes its way to the surface." Thom felt good being able to pull that rabbit out of his hat.

"I still don't get it," Charlotte said.

The view made Charlotte and Bella feel small. It seemed to erase any notion of stress or anxiety. Bella frequently fell into vortexes of anxiety. It usually began with a stressful or controversial situation. When she heard about death, disease, injustice, or anything else temperamental, her heart would race, and trigger a desire to fight anything or anyone. These hikes allowed her to take her aggression out on the paths of the most beautiful national park in Canada, and perhaps the world. Her mind was at ease, and she could breathe with regularity. The sweat, the pain, the exhaustion put her mind in a good place; she told herself she wouldn't get upset at frivolous things anymore. "I have never felt this good, Dad," she said with a smile.

"I feel the same way, Bella-bean," Thom responded as he took a bite from a granola bar.

"Did Mom feel this good when she was here?" Bella asked.

"Your Mom and I never wanted to leave this place. We loved this mountain. We had our first kiss here." Thom pointed to the gondola on the other side of the boardwalk.

"What?!" Charlotte shouted.

"First kiss? Are you serious?" Bella was shocked.

"We climbed Sulphur on our third date. I gave her a special birthday card when we made it here. She opened it, smiled, leaned in, and kissed me. It was the greatest day of my life."

"Gross," said Charlotte.

"As a guy, I always had to make the first move, but your Mom leaned in before I could even realize what was happening. I thought to myself, this was the woman I was going to be with for the rest of my life," Thom said with spirit.

The three finished their snacks and made their way into the building where the giftshop and washrooms were located. It shocked the girls that they were able to build a giant structure like this atop a mountain. The three meandered through the gift shop and read the various posters outlining the history of Sulphur and Banff National Park.

Charlotte learned about James Hector, and how he was exploring routes for the national railroad. His horse ran away and in the pursuit, Hector was kicked in the chest with the horse's leg. His companions thought he was dead, so they dug a grave and right as they were about to put him in the hole, he regained consciousness. The pass and nearby river were subsequently called Kicking Horse Pass and Kicking Horse River.

Bella read about the Brewster Brothers, and their pioneering journey from Ireland escaping the potato famine in the 19th century. Bella pondered the time-period and how it was a much simpler, but much harder time. She was inspired by the Brewsters and how innovative and entrepreneurial they were. They started providing Banff with guided tours, they raised cattle and created outfitting operations throughout North America as their family expanded. Bella was inspired by their ability to make it in Banff without T.V., the internet or automobiles; they drudged through the mountains on horseback and raised their children on their backs.

While his girls were intently reading the posters about the building, Thom couldn't help but think about the night before and how much fun he had with Lacy and her friends. He wondered if Lacy loved to climb as much as he did. He felt a childlike giddiness come over him.

"Dad, look at this guy," Charlotte beckoned Thom to where she was looking at a poster of 'Wild Bill' Peyto.

The picture of 'Wild Bill' on the poster was a stoic one. He was a unique looking character. He was smoking a cigar, wearing a sombrero, kerchief, and buckskin coat with a fringe border. He looked like he valued Banff and his personal space.

Thom read the poster and affirmed his thoughts about the rough-looking character. Apparently in the mid-1890s, on a Saturday night he walked into a crowded Banff hotel with a live lynx strapped to his back. A few moments later he found himself alone in the bar, just as he preferred.

"Quite the cowboy, eh Char?" Thom nudged Charlotte.

"He kind of looks like you," Charlotte nudged her dad back.

"He was certainly a lot tougher than me."

The two shared a laugh as they looked over to Bella who was browsing the keychains in the gift shop. There were wood keychains, metal keychains, glass keychains, animal keychains, numbers, letters, and anything else you could possibly imagine. Bella loved collecting keychains and decided on one with a picture of the gondola on it. It was not only significant because it would always remind her of today, but also where her mom and dad had their first kiss. It felt like this gondola played a role in her and her sister's creation.

Bella made her way to the cash register and paid for the keychain with a twenty-dollar bill as Charlotte and Thom made their way to the giftshop.

"What'd you get, what'd you get?" Charlotte asked.

"Just a keychain," Bella nonchalantly responded.

Eventually the three made their way onto the gondola that carried them down the mountain. It was nerve-racking at first, but the girls gave into trust as they descended over the treetops. After a long hike it was nice just to take in the views from above. The ride was only a few minutes, but it was relaxing and full of memorable scenery.

As the gondola car descended, Bella thought about the connection made between her parents at the top of Sulphur Mountain and how she might, one day, lean in and kiss somebody that was special too.

Chapter 4 – Townhall

Townhall was a relatively new modern building. Its architecture was a combination of a classic wood lodge building with modern concrete formations. It was a two-story structure with large wooden support posts around the perimeter of the building. Welcoming steps lead past a flagpole and gardens to a door with a wooden sign that read 'Townhall.' It was a nice place to work with excellent energy.

The employees at Banff townhall were always in great spirits. There wasn't a lot of room to be moody when governing within a national park. It was a great working environment. The municipality of Banff was unique as it was run by both the federal and local government because it was both a national park and a town of 8000 people.

There were always a lot of seasonal employees, gardeners, snow removal, tour guides, ski lift operators, forestry workers, and hotel staff. There were always new faces about townhall. Lacy was a permanent resident and had lived in Banff since she moved from Calgary.

Today it was business as usual. Her office had a large desk covered in books, blueprints, and other random papers. She had hand carved wood sculptures, tribal masks, and other trinkets that gave her working environment colour and character. People loved visiting Lacy's office. She always had drinks, snacks, and loads of entertaining conversation pieces. It was a place that brought Lacy joy.

Her current project was a small hotel redevelopment and parking lot that needed to reconnect to all the city services. She still loved to use the drafting table in her office. Putting pencil to paper allowed her to go through all the motions of architecture. Many new architects were strictly using AutoCAD and shied away from pencil and paper. Lacy was determined to continue with the way she was taught and the way she could be the most creative with her ideas.

As Lacy was busy at her desk, there was a knock at her door.

"Come in," Lacy shouted.

Tammy and Barb were at the door with big smiles on their faces.

"Are you busy?" Barb asked.

"Can we come in?" Tammy added.

"Sure, yeah, come in, come in," invited Lacy.

"Did you have a good time on Friday with Thom?" Barb coyly asked. "He's kind of cute."

"Oh sure, he's great. It's too bad he lives in Ontario," Lacy said.

"Oh, who cares. Go get laid, Lace," Barb added.

"Relax Barb," Tammy laughed.

"What? She hasn't got her freak on since last year, when that cowboy came in from Red Deer," Barb said imitating a bow-legged cowboy.

"He was from Medicine Hat, he was very attractive, and he was not a cowboy," Lacy corrected.

"Wherever he's from, Regina, Moose Factory, or Whitehorse, you should show a little interest in Tommy Gun." Barb's tone sounded like a therapist. "He's a great guy. He's wounded. He could use a woman's breast to lay on."

"What the hell is that supposed to mean?" Lacy quipped.

"You both look good together. You're both clearly attracted to each other and you both scream 'I haven't been laid in years'. Use it or lose it, Lace," Barb rebounded.

"You are making me sick to my stomach," Lacy said.

"Can we go to lunch? I'm starving," Tammy pleaded.

The three ladies made their way to a little lunch spot that served the best sandwiches. Bernice's Sammies baked their own fresh bread and always had the freshest ingredients, despite being in the middle of the Rocky Mountains. Bernice took great pride in making sandwiches for the business workers in Banff. They all knew her by name and often asked her to cater events around town. She rolled her own meatballs, shaved her own ham, and hand cut every vegetable at her disposal.

The three ladies generally ordered the same thing when they went to Bernice's. Tammy always ordered the AAA Alberta roast beef on rye, Barb ordered the ham and cheddar on white, and Lacy ordered the chicken breast on whole wheat. If it wasn't their favourite meal of the week, it was certainly close.

"Will it be the usual, ladies?" Bernice asked, dressed in a hairnet and white apron.

All three friends nodded in affirmation. "You betcha," said Lacy.

"We are starving," Barb added.

Bernice gave them all a warm smile and began preparing their sandwiches. The three ladies grabbed the lone table at the front window of Bernice's and stared outside at the busy main street of Banff.

In Banff, very few people had televisions and those that did, hardly watched them. It was a scenic town where, on any given day, you might see a herd of elk or a band of mountain goats walking down the side of the road. The mountains and landscape were alive; snow covered the mountains at different times of year, weather changed abruptly, rivers raged, and people from all over the world walked the streets. Lacy, Barb, and Tammy were people-watching and noticed, what appeared to be, a Swedish supermodel convention walk by.

Barb scoffed. "Whores."

"Skanks," added Tammy.

"There must be an anorexia convention in town," Lacy joked as the blonde group passed by.

The three ladies then noticed an older, short couple across the street dressed in earthy tones, overalls, Birkenstocks, and matching fedora hats.

"They must be from middle earth," Lacy said.

"What's middle earth?" asked Tammy.

"It's near the equator," joked Barb.

"Hmm," said Tammy, who was still confused.

"It's not near the equator, it's a land filled with magic, dragons and hobbits," Lacy described.

"What's a hobbit?" asked Tammy.

"Those are hobbits," Lacy quipped.

Tammy still didn't get the joke. Tolkien was about as far removed as satellite technology to Tammy. Lacy thought it was funny and wondered if Thom would get her middle-earth humour.

Once the hobbit-folk passed by, a young couple strolled past the front window. The two youngsters were holding hands and laughing without a care in the world. The boy wore torn jeans, a white shirt, and a flannel top tied around his waist. The girl wore a jean skirt with a green vest and a hat with a flower on it.

"It's Blossom and Joey!" yelled Barb.

"Whoa." added Tammy.

All three ladies shared a laugh. This had been a ritual for years now and it never grew old. Banff was the perfect place to people-watch. People were always coming and going, styles were always changing, and languages were unique and diverse.

Just as Bernice was finishing up putting the toppings on the sandwiches, Thom and his two daughters strolled by.

"Hey, isn't that Thom?" asked Barb.

"Those must be his two daughters. Aren't they pretty." Tammy added.

"It looks like they're both coming back from a hike. I'm going to pop my head out and say…" Barb got up to leave.

"Wait!" shouted Lacy, which froze Barb in her tracks. "I don't think he wants to…"

Barb interrupted Lacy: "Nonsense!" She opened the door. "Hey, Thom!"

Thom spun his head to the sandwich shop and saw Barb's head sticking out the door.

"Oh, hi Barb!" Thom fired back.

"Are you three hungry? Bernice has the best sandwiches in western Canada," said the head sticking out of the door.

"I could eat," Bella interjected.

Charlotte looked at her dad. "Same."

"Sure, we could eat," Thom said.

Thom, Bella, and Charlotte made their way into Bernice's and the first thing that caught Thom's eye was that Lacy was with them. She was dressed business casual, but he thought she looked amazing. He was slightly self-conscious because of the sweat rolling down his forehead and his enormous pit stains from the Sulphur climb.

"Hi Thom!" Lacy said in a welcoming voice. "These must be your daughters."

"Yes, this is Charlotte and Bella. Say hello girls."

"Hello," Bella said.

"Hi," Charlotte mumbled.

Both girls hated meeting new people, especially those born before 1980. Like most teenagers, they thought anyone in their twenties or older were dinosaurs.

"Nice to meet you both. Your dad has told us so much about you," Lacy said.

"This is Barb, Tammy, and Lacy," Thom introduced the three ladies to his daughters. "We met yesterday and had some coffee and donuts after the hike."

"Yeah, I had like seven donuts. I was feeling ill this morning," joked Tammy.

"Yeah, I shouldn't have had that last coffee. I was up all night," added Barb winking at Thom.

"You went out last night?" asked Bella.

"Yeah, you both were sound asleep when I left."

"Your dad said you just graduated high school, Bella. Congratulations," Lacy said with a smile.

Bella smiled back and turned to her father staring at Lacy. Bella started to put the pieces together, sensing her dad might have a crush on her. Never, in a million years, did she think her dad would ever look at another woman. The thought gave Bella a rush of anxiety.

"Yeah, I did," Bella responded, then switched topics abruptly. "We are only here for a couple weeks, then back home to Toronto."

Lacy could sense her territoriality and understood the teenager's anxiety and quickly changed the topic conversation again. "Are you ready for the best sandwich you've ever had?"

"I am starving. We're just coming down from the Sulphur Mountain gondola. We had some snacks, but nothing substantial," Thom said.

Thom, Charlotte, and Bella ordered sandwiches as Bernice delivered Barb, Tammy, and Lacy's lunch. They all shared a jovial lunchtime conversation. Tammy and Barb made the girls laugh and feel welcome and avoided any awkwardness that surrounded Thom and Lacy.

Everyone enjoyed their sandwiches and expressed their gratitude to Bernice and her little establishment. They all got up and made their way back outside.

"I have a great idea," Lacy said. "Bella, Charlotte, do you want to have a spa day tomorrow with the ladies and I? That is, if it's okay with your dad?"

"I've never been to a spa before," Charlotte said.

"It's great. Mud baths, facials, massages…You'll both love it," Tammy said encouragingly.

"Do you like golf? You remember Rob, Jeff, and Peter, well I know they usually go golfing when we go to the spa. Maybe you could join their foursome tomorrow while the girls come with us for a lady's afternoon," Lacy suggested.

"That sounds fun. What do you think girls?" Thom asked Bella and Charlotte.

"Excellent," Charlotte said as she gave an enthusiastic thumbs up.

"Alright, whatever. Going to a strange spa with complete strangers sounds perfectly safe," mumbled Bella.

"Great! Here's Rob's number. Give him a call and tell him the plan. I'm sure he'd love for you to join them," Lacy said.

All were enthusiastic about their plans as they all parted ways. Thom and the girls made their way back to the lodge to relax for the night, while Lacy, Barb, and Tammy went back to townhall.

Lacy felt slightly nervous about the thought of spending a few hours with a relative stranger's kids, but she knew they would love it and it would give Thom a few hours to air it out with the boys. After all, she remembered what it was like to hang out with only your dad for days at a time.

When they arrived back at the townhall, Lacy couldn't help but feel thankful she still had her mother, even though she was a few hours away. She thought about her final years at high school and her first years at university and how they were filled with memories of her mother's support. Lacy's mother would cook meals for her and her friends, she would lend Lacy money, take her shopping, and be an active listener whenever Lacy had to get something off her chest. June Clark, Lacy's mom, was a devoted mother, wife, and friend. Lacy felt overwhelming sympathy for both Charlotte and Bella as they were now without a mother who would provide such support.

The Clark family was a big one. Lacy was the youngest of five children and the only girl. June drove the kids everywhere, the boys to hockey and lacrosse and Lacy to figure skating, dance, and basketball. There were also plenty of grandbabies for June to spoil. Lacy absolutely dreaded the idea of not having her around and was being overcome with compassion for Thom's girls.

Once back at her desk, she looked out the window then at her telephone. She picked it up and dialled a number. A few rings later, someone picked up and said 'hello.' Lacy smiled.

"Hi, Mom. It's great to hear your voice. Just calling to see how you're doing and to say how much I love you."

Chapter 5 - Wellness Day

The Banff Springs Golf Course was at the base of a mountain along with the Fairmount Hotel. It was a beautiful course and location for people to get upset while whacking a little white ball around. Thom hated golf growing up but grew to love it in his thirties. It was incredibly difficult for him at first, and frustrating; divot, shank, hook, slice, worm-burn. It was a steep learning curve, at first. Interlock your grip, keep your head still, bend your knees, stay relaxed, through the ball, it all seemed too much, but as the years went by, he seemed to start putting the pieces together and hit the ball with more consistency.

Val hated golf, one of the reasons Thom rarely went. 'It's a waste of time and money,' Val would say. And it would only lead to Thom coming home in a state of rage. But now, in 1998, it took his mind off the pain he was going through with the passing of his late wife. It got him off the couch and into the elements. You had to be completely present in golf, your mind had to be free and clear.

Rob, Jeff, and Pete all loved golf. Tiger Woods was fresh on the scene and totally flipped the sporting world on its head. The year before, Tiger had won the Masters at 21, turning the heads of the old guard and every cigar-smoking guy on tour. Jeff always bought Tiger Woods apparel. It seemed ridiculous, but he thought it gave him the edge. Rob loved Tiger, but was always trying to copy his swing, which would throw off any type of consistency he had been having. Pete was the pessimist. He thought Tiger's father was too hard on him and all the recent success was too much too soon for the young golfer. Pete would often say that Tiger was getting lucky, or he might develop a drug problem, or the PGA would find he was somehow cheating.

The foursome found themselves on the course on another beautiful day in Banff, full sunshine with only partial cloudiness. They shared a couple of baskets on the driving range to help warm up their swings. Thom got out his driver to start, thinking that it was the easiest club to hit, but at the same time would impress Jeff, Pete, and Rob. He strapped on his glove, interlocked his grip, and stepped up to the ball. He took a deep breath and envisioned himself on the 18th hole of Augusta with a one-shot lead. Into his back swing and through the ball, Thom swung with all his might and knocked the ball five feet in front of him. Rob, Jeff, and Pete all laughed.

"Swinging a little too hard there, Tiger," Jeff said.

"Nice and easy," Pete added.

"Yeah, it's been a while," Thom felt stupid. "New clubs too."

"Right," Rob said sarcastically.

It took a few swings to shed the nerves and warm up, but eventually Thom started to feel good. He started to correct his slice and eventually started hitting the ball straight as an arrow. The three other guys all had nice swings and were hitting their drives 250 yards or farther.

"So, have you ever golfed here, Thom?" asked Pete.

"No, never had the chance. But Jesus, what a great course. So scenic," Thom replied.

"It's a beauty. Only problem you might run into is a herd of elk on the fairway," Rob said.

"How are the greens?" asked Thom.

"They're fast. Good drainage and well maintained," answered Pete.

"So, Thom, do you want to take a cart or walk it?" asked Jeff.

"A day like this; I don't mind walking. How about you guys?" Thom responded.

"Let's walk it," said Rob.

All four guys agreed on walking the beautiful course surrounded by mountains. As they made their way from hole to hole the air seemed to get purer, the green background got greener, and the rivers became clearer. When the four got to the tee box of the 15th hole they saw a herd of about 50 elk in the middle of the fairway.

"Would you take a look at that," Thom said as he saw the herd.

"They love grazing on the fairways in the summertime," Jeff said.

"Do they move?" Thom asked.

"Only when they're ready," Rob responded.

Thom was okay with waiting and enjoying the scenery, plus he wasn't exactly winning the round against the other guys. Thom was used to seeing deer from Ontario that would bolt at the first sign of human activity, but these elk clearly weren't afraid of them. Thom wondered why. Then he started to put the pieces together. This was a national park and hunting was not permitted, so the elk have probably figured it out that they're safe within a certain area, and, as a bonus, there was fresh Kentucky bluegrass on demand.

There were about a dozen spring calves that never moved far from their mothers. They seemed to know in the first year of life they were in danger from wolves, grizzly bears, black bears, and cougars. Thom admired the herd and hierarchy of the tournament species. Definitely not a pair-bonding species like humans, Thom thought.

Pete was totalling up the scores on the scorecard, while Jeff and Rob sat on a nearby bench smoking cigars.

"Pete is the leader, Rob two strokes behind, Jeff 4 strokes behind and Thom…12 shots behind," Pete said.

"Yeah, thanks for reminding me I'm terrible," Thom responded.

"So, Thom, when are you going back to Toronto?" asked Jeff.

"In about 10 days," Thom said. "But each day I'm here, I don't want to leave."

"Yeah, the novelty wears off after a while, but it's beautiful and there's never a shortage of things to do," Jeff said.

"Calgary's close, Jasper and Edmonton aren't too far off either," added Rob.

"Yeah, it's great here. Things sure have changed since 1977 and in some ways, things haven't changed at all," Thom reflected.

"You were here in 1977?" asked Rob.

"I met my late wife here that summer of '77. That's why my daughters and I came here, so I could show them where we met and first started dating. You know, the sentimental journey," Thom explained.

"Sorry to hear about your wife, Thom. What happened to her if you don't mind me asking?" Jeff said sincerely.

"She got gallbladder cancer and battled for a couple of years until she passed away last winter, a year and a half ago. It's been tough on all of us, especially the girls. But I figured this trip would help in the grieving process," Thom explained.

"I don't mean to get too personal, but have they been seeing a therapist?" Pete asked earnestly.

Thom was thankful he asked. "Yeah, it's been helpful. The toughest thing for the girls, especially Charlotte, was seeing the transformation of their mother into a ghost of her former self. Pretty awful for a young girl to experience."

"I couldn't imagine," Pete replied.

"You're doing all the right things, Thom. It's gotta be tough for you too," Jeff said.

"We were married 19 years. Mother of my children. Love of my life. Now we are trying to sell the house and move out of the place the kids grew up in. It's tough for them living in an environment where every corner reminds them of their mother," Thom explained.

"Any luck finding a house? How's the housing market right now in Ontario?" Pete asked.

"It keeps going up. Hopefully, I should be able to sell it quick. We should probably get some solid offers," Thom said optimistically.

Rob looked out to the fairway on the 15th hole. "Looks like the herd is moving on," he said as the herd moved into the forest at the side of the fairway. The four guys made their way to the tee box and continued their round.

At the spa, Bella, Charlotte, Lacy, Tammy, and Barb were just arriving at the wellness centre and spa. Tammy had called beforehand and made reservations for the five ladies to receive the complete care package. The premium service included a 60-minute massage, basalt hot stones, warm oil scalp therapy and a detox foot scrub.

Charlotte and Bella were full of nerves because they had no idea of what to expect. They had never had a massage, let alone a detox foot scrub. Barb, Tammy, and Lacy had been there on several occasions and were all on a first name basis with the staff and management. This was usually the best part of the week for the ladies who kept reassuring Bella and Charlotte they were in for a lovely surprise.

Once inside, Bella and Charlotte couldn't help but notice how clean and fresh everything seemed. Toronto businesses were sometimes in 150-year-old houses that had any number of combinations of mould, water damage, bed bugs, cockroaches, mice, or rats. This place seemed brand new and smelled like a winter cedarwood forest. Besides the interior, the staff were friendly and positive, unlike most employees working within Toronto.

Bella turned and whispered to Charlotte: "I can't believe how nice people are here. It kind of makes me sick."

"Is this what people are supposed to be like?" Charlotte whispered back.

The five ladies followed the staff receptionist into the change room and began preparing for the initial 60-minute massage.

"This place is amazing," Bella said to the ladies.

Lacy responded to Bella's amazement, "It never grows old, Bella. We've been coming here for ten years now, and it never ceases to amaze."

"You have to try the tea," Tammy said with a smile.

"What is it?" Charlotte asked.

Just as the receptionist was leaving the room, she turned and said: "It's a handcrafted blend of pure white tea, rosebuds, and jasmine pearls. It relaxes the mind and arouses the senses, making it the perfect aromatherapy blend."

"She's good," Barb said as the receptionist left the changing room.

After the ladies got changed into the white robes, they made their way into the massage room where there were five masseuses waiting with their arms crossed in front of them. Each lady climbed aboard a massage table and laid down face first.

Once the massages began, all five ladies began to groan in a symphony of delight.

"This is extremely amazing," Charlotte moaned.

Everyone, including the masseuses started laughing.

Rob, Jeff, Pete, and Thom finished up their putts on the 18th hole and walked their way to the clubhouse. The exterior of the clubhouse was a marvel, but the interior took it to a different level.

The dining room was circular in design with 30-foot ceilings and a large round stone fireplace in the middle of the room. Above the fireplace were large Ojibway Chief heads that were hand carved. The fireplace certainly was the focal point of the room, as it commanded attention and respect.

Glass windows surrounded the entire room letting in an abundance of natural light which made you feel as though you were outside. Thom was in awe of the architectural specs of the place, as he often took note of structural and design elements. He loved it when interior spaces welcomed natural light. In his own home he had two bay windows. This room felt uniquely special. The mountains in the background, the Bow River meandering through the pass, and the interior of the clubhouse combined for an experience that he would never forget.

The four men sat at a table near the window overlooking the bright blue Bow River. The table had silverware, water glasses, and menus to browse. Within a minute of the guys sitting down, a young waitress came to the table.

"Good afternoon gentlemen. How was your round?" the waitress asked.

"Not very special," Thom quickly remarked.

Pete was totalling up the scorecard. "It looks like I won by two strokes, gentlemen."

"Congratulations," said the waitress. "What was your score?"

"I had an 81, Rob 83, Jeff 86 and Thom…there's a lot of maths here…and Thom 104," Pete cheekily remarked.

Everyone shared a laugh.

"I'm surprised you can count that high," Rob joked.

"Would you care to start with something refreshing to drink?" asked the waitress.

"A pitcher of your finest with four glasses, please," said Rob.

"Is Banff Springs Lager okay with you gentlemen?"

"Perfect," said Rob.

The waitress left to go get the drinks.

"104?" asked Thom. "Are you sure you got that right?"

"Yeah, I had to use a calculator, because my brain can't compute that many numbers," Pete said.

"Funny," Thom said sarcastically. "Are you guys going to order some food?"

"I certainly am. Thom, try the steak sandwich. It's great. You'll love it," Jeff remarked.

"I'm going for a burger and fries," Pete announced.

"Same," Rob followed.

"So, Thom, are you loving Banff?" asked Pete.

"I love this place. It's special to me. Only a couple days into my vacation and I feel younger already," Thom replied.

"What else do you have planned?" asked Jeff.

"We're going to the hot springs possibly tomorrow. We are going to take a trip to Calgary to do some shopping, head to Lake Louise and maybe head to the interior for a couple days. I want to take the girls up Cascade too, but I'm not quite sure they're up for it. I guess I'll wait and see."

"Yeah, that's a tough one. It's fairly sheer and a lot of loose rocks," said Rob.

"It's got a false summit too," added Jeff. "Tricky up there."

"I think it's about 10 km. Just bring enough water and don't try to take shortcuts or go off trail. Pretty dangerous mountain if you're not careful," Pete warned.

"So, you said your girls are almost ready for university. Have they thought about it or made any decisions yet?" asked Jeff.

"They have no clue. Bella, my oldest, does likes business, Charlotte likes the Backstreet Boys. So, it is up in the air at this point," Thom said laughing.

"What's keeping you in Ontario?" asked Jeff.

"Well, Valerie's parents are still in Ottawa and mine are in North Bay, so there's that. Val's passing threw the girls into a downward spiral. We've all been seeing a therapist to help with the healing. It certainly has been a process," Thom explained.

"Come out to Alberta," Jeff exclaimed.

"West is best," Rob added.

"It's something I might actually consider," Thom added.

"You could find work, I'm sure. The only thing you really must worry about out here are grizzly bears...and I have spray for that," Rob joked.

"Thanks for the idea. I could climb mountains, live the clean life," Thom said.

As they were all sharing a laugh, the waitress returned with the pitcher of lager and four glasses. "Did you want to order some food?" the waitress asked as she poured the beer.

"Two burgers, two steak sandwiches, all four with fries," Pete ordered.

"Great!" the waitress said as she poured the final glass.

"Cheers, here's to my new friends planting seeds for the future!" Thom said with a grin.

The four chinked their glasses together and took a drink of the cold delicious beer.

The five ladies felt intoxicated after 60 long minutes of deep tissue massage. Their eyes seemed glossy and often rolled toward the back of their heads as a result of their relaxed muscles and tissues.

"My muscles seem so relaxed," said Tammy.

"I feel like I'm on the moon," Lacy added.

"Does any else feel drunk?" Barb asked.

"I feel really light-headed," said Charlotte.

"That's because you're an airhead," joked Bella.

The girls all sat down in the leather chairs that were in the next room. They were greeted by another employee of the spa bringing tea.

"Welcome, take some time to unwind after the massage, and when you're ready, head to this next room for the hot basalt stone treatment," said the employee as she poured five teas.

"Hot stones? That sounds like medieval torture," Bella said.

"The heat from the basalt stones deeply penetrate the muscular structures, soothing and releasing tension and toxins, warming and sedating the body's systems," the employee added.

"Regardless, it makes me nervous," Bella said as the employee left the ladies alone.

"So, your dad says you're off to university next year, Bella?" Lacy inquired.

"Yeah, I got accepted to the Ryerson, York, and U of T. I'm not quite sure where I want to go, but I'm going to check out the campuses when I get back to Ontario," Bella answered.

"You don't sound terribly excited," Lacy replied.

"Bella really wants to travel for a year," Charlotte interjected.

"Dad doesn't want me taking a gap year, because he figures I won't go back to school when it's over," Bella explained.

"That is good advice. A lot of people don't go back to school after a gap year. But there is a ton of people who do. There's really no sense in dumping a bunch of money into education that you're not sure about. Some of the most interesting people I know still don't know what they want to do," Lacy said.

"I want to get into a science field, maybe biology or chemistry or something," Bella said.

"Those are pretty demanding programs, Bella," Lacy said.

"It's stressful at this point. I want to experience adventure and travel, but at the same time I do want to go to school, eventually," Bella explained.

"Whatever you choose to do, I'm sure it will be the right decision," Lacy said.

"Yeah, I've got some decisions to make soon," Bella said.

"What are you thinking about after high school, Charlotte?" asked Lacy.

"Well, not quite sure yet. I like building things. I like cooking. I like art. I like reading. I also like science, history, and math," Charlotte rambled.

"Well, it sounds like you love pretty much everything," said Tammy.

"I'm just not quite sure yet," Charlotte said.

"Bella, Charlotte, if there's any advice I can give you, it's to take your time; listen to your instincts. It may seem ultra stressful because it's what the world has pushed for so long. Do well in school, get straight A's, go to college, get a job, get married, get a house, have a family. It's okay to feel things out instead of jumping straight into the deep end. I know some people that took some courses in first year university and then totally switched directions and ended up in an entirely different program." Lacy told this story as if it were someone else, but it was her own experience.

Lacy went to the University of Alberta for medical sciences but dropped out and enrolled in architecture school the next year. She always listened to her instincts. In her first year at U of A, she was miserable. She hated being surrounded by ultra-competitive med students from around the world. Most of the students were not sociable, they were short, abrasive, and rude. There wasn't one person from that year she remembered, except the rude, arrogant professor who thought he was the smartest man in the world and wouldn't give her the time of day.

Once enrolling in architecture school, she found her groove. She loved designing, she loved the brilliant architects and structures they created. She found such joy in Frank Lloyd Wright and Le Corbusier. She remembers the first time she saw Fallingwater and remembers the blending of architecture and the natural environment; the water seemed to flow through the house without the distractive reminders of modern construction. She also remembers seeing the Maison Blanche, built for Le Corbusier's parents in La Chaux-de-Fonds when she was 22 years old.

Lacy saw a lot of herself in Bella and Charlotte, full of enthusiasm and interest in all things. She recognized in Bella all the stresses she felt when deciding on university.

"Maybe you do need a year to work and travel. It could help clarify any doubts you are having about what career path you want to follow," Lacy added.

"Yeah, it's all kind of up in the air right now," Bella said frowning.

"I wouldn't worry, kiddo. You're smart, you'll figure it out," Barb encouraged.

"How did you know what you wanted to do?" asked Bella.

"I had to make some mistakes first," Lacy said earnestly.

"I loved talking on the phone and taking messages, so the transition to being a secretary was natural," said Barb.

"I just loved being nosey and talking on the phone, so Barb got me a job," Tammy said jokingly.

The five ladies were having a blast. They shared stories about boys, road trips, period problems, travel plans, and new beauty products. It was a memorable experience for Bella and Charlotte, as they had never been around a group of grown women and had such casual, R-rated conversations.

At the Banff Springs Clubhouse, the guys munched their food in silence. The only audible sounds were a series of moans and groans. Even when the waitress came to do a quality check, they said nothing, as their mouths were full, they just nodded their heads in affirmation. Thom was the first one to take a break from stuffing his mouth. "God damn, I had to come up for a breath."

"Mmm," said Jeff.

"Mmm," followed Rob.

"This has to be the best sandwich I've ever had," Thom said.

"If you want me to finish yours, just let me know," Pete said.

"No, no, don't be silly," Thom replied.

The five girls were all face down on their designated tables as various employees placed hot stones on their vertebrates of the ladies. With each stone placed, the ladies would react differently. 'Eeps,' 'oohs,' 'ahhhs,' 'owwws,' were heard overlapping one another. Charlotte seemed to be enjoying it the most, as she was completely silent as the stones were placed along her spine.

The employees placing the hot stones found the whole thing amusing, as the ladies were lying face down and making noises like those coming from a barnyard.

The guys had finished their meals and clearly, eating too fast had affected their ability to sit up straight. All four of them had their hands placed on their bulging stomachs.

"If I smoked, this would be the time to have one," said Jeff.

"I feel pregnant," said Rob.

"I'm having trouble speaking and I think I'm losing my eyesight," Pete said.

"Anyone for dessert?" asked Thom. Everyone shared a laugh as clearly not one of them wanted to think about food. "Thanks for inviting me out with you guys today. I can't believe how welcomed you've made me feel," he said to his new friends.

"No problem. I remember Toronto being the loneliest place in the world. Five million people and yet you felt completely alone," said Pete.

"Yeah, it feels completely different since Valerie's passing a year and a half ago. We used to be a lot more involved in the community, but we hardly go anywhere anymore," Thom said.

"Yeah, you're getting over a major tragedy, Thom. Like anything, it's going to take time for the wounds to heal. Same with your daughters," Rob said genuinely.

"Tomorrow's a new day, my friend," Jeff added.

"Well said guys. Thanks for your support," Thom replied.

At the spa, the girls were now getting the warm oil scalp treatment. They were all laying on their backs with cucumbers placed over their eyes. With each move, the girls moaned as their heads were massaged with hot soothing oil.

"This feels so good," moaned Charlotte.

"I want to do this every day," Bella remarked.

"I want to live here," Charlotte one-upped her sister.

"I want to live, eat, and work here," Bella trumped.

"That's gross," Charlotte said giving her best stink-face. "Hot oil and cucumber sandwiches."

"You're an idiot," Bella snipped.

"Don't call me that!" Charlotte yelled.

The guys were now in the parking lot of the Banff Springs Golf Club. Thom admired the massive building they had just left. It was a unique looking building, somewhat resembling an alien spacecraft. They loaded two different cars with their clubs and gears. They changed their shoes into more comfortable sandals and flip flops.

Thom loved the way he felt after golf. There was always something to think about. Though most of the round was frustrating, he always pulled a few good things out of the madness. Today it was about his follow-through and how he needed to swing through the ball. Jeff was giving Thom a ride back to his lodge, while Pete was driving Rob.

"See you guys soon," Pete waved.

"Thanks guys, what a blast," Thom replied.

Thom got into the car and took a deep breath and smiled. Jeff got in and noticed the grin on Thom's face. "What are you thinking about?"

"Probably the most memorable round I've ever had," Thom said, still smiling.

Jeff backed out of the parking space, and they made their way downtown.

"What are you and your girls up to tomorrow?" Jeff casually asked.

"I'm taking the girls into Calgary for some shopping and a Stampeders game."

"Football, eh. Do they like football?"

"Charlotte thinks the Calgary Stampeders are cowboys who work at the stampede," Thom said with a giggle.

"Haha. It's too bad you and the girls aren't going to be here for the Stampede. It's usually a gong show," Jeff said.

"Yeah, maybe another year. Vacations fly by," Thom said.

"Never enough time," Jeff said.

"You said it." Thom laid his head back against the headrest and looked out onto the Bow River as they cruised between the pines back to Banff.

The ladies walked with jelly-legs through the parking lot. The sun was bright, and the air was warm as they strode with euphoric smiles on their faces.

"Thanks for the great spa day. This was fantastic," said Bella.

"It's no problem. It's been a pleasure," Tammy responded. "Let us know if you ever want to do this again."

Though hanging out with 35-year-olds wasn't exactly cool, it was a lot of fun for Bella and Charlotte as they laughed, mingled, and relaxed with Lacy, Tammy, and Barb. It had been a long time since Bella could loosen up and genuinely laugh with friends. Her back was up for so long; postured against letting loose, being goofy, singing songs, snorting at jokes, and just being herself.

Her closest friends kept her at arm's length since her mom's passing. She had become snappy, mean, and cruel and her friends felt it the most. Part of her grieving process was learning she couldn't treat people with such intolerance, especially her loyal friends. Bella stood her friend Elisa up for three straight weekends, she quit math club and told the group they were all 'try-hards', and she dumped her boyfriend at the time because he was talking with another girl at school about a chemistry problem. Bella was temperamental and easily offended throughout her mother's illness;

anything that could possibly offend her, did so. Throughout therapy her self-reflections and journals reminded her to be kind and open to communication.

Charlotte, on the other hand, withdrew from all social engagements and fell completely silent and numb. She had friends, but not many as her reclusiveness increased. She loved sports, but stopped playing, blaming everything from injury to work. She once loved the community she felt in theatre but stopped all her commitments. The only person she truly was open with, the year following her mother's death, was her sister. Therapy taught Charlotte how to trust again. This day at the spa was an excellent exercise in trust.

All the excitement and physical exercise was certainly helping both of the girls keep their mind on positive things. They felt very little anxiety and depression in the mountain air. Both girls found their shoulders relaxed and the different pains and stresses leaving their necks and heads.

Thom was dropped off at the lodge around the same time the girls were. They met up inside their room. Besides the casual pleasantries and greetings, they were all too tired to engage in any meaningful conversation. Each took their turn in the shower and curled up on their beds for a long nap.

Bella woke around 6:00pm and was starving. She shook her sister who was seemingly in the middle of a good dream. "Wake up. I'm starving. Let's go get something to eat."

Charlotte was clearly not impressed. "Would you bugger off. I was just about to kiss Brad Pitt."

"Dad! I'm hungry!" Bella yelled.

Thom opened his eyes slowly and smiled at the ceiling. "Sure thing. Let's go down to the dining room and see what's on special."

The three got changed and made their way down to the packed dining room. The restaurant had a wonderful smell of garlic, gravy, and prime rib. Thom licked his lips with anticipation. He loved a nice jus with prime rib and mashed potatoes. Though the steak sandwich he had earlier was filling, he had quickly regained his appetite. His metabolism was speeding up with all the extra walking and exercise. He was feeling younger by the day.

The first thing Bella did when she sat down was look for Brody. She spun around a few times; looking over her and her sister's shoulder.

"What are you looking for?" Thom said smiling.

"She's looking for her new boyfriend," Charlotte said with a smirk.

"Boyfriend?" Thom laughed.

"Obviously not my boyfriend," Bella said defensively.

"He works here at the restaurant," Charlotte added.

"He's a cute boy I talked to. So what?" Bella said as she once again looked around to ensure he wasn't behind her.

The waitress came over and the three each ordered prime rib and mashed potatoes and a ginger ale. As they ordered, Thom's mouth began to water as he anticipated the soon-to-arrive red meat.

As the waitress walked away from the table, Brody appeared from the kitchen carrying two plates he delivered to another table. Charlotte was the first to notice him.

"There he is," Charlotte snickered.

"Hard working boy," Thom joked.

"Will both of you shut up," Bella snapped.

After Brody delivered the food, he made his way over to Thom's table.

"He's coming over," Thom leaned and whispered to Bella.

Bella could do nothing but stare down at the table as she flushed red with embarrassment.

"Hi Bella," Brody said as he passed by their table. "Busy night."

"Hi Brody," Bella was at a loss for words. "Keep working hard!"

"Keep working hard?" Charlotte whispered to Bella. "That's all you could think of?"

"Leave your uncomfortable sister alone, Char," Thom said with a grin.

"I'm going to murder both of you in your sleep tonight," Bella said with an evil furrowed brow.

"I wanted to talk to you girls about tomorrow," Thom said to change the subject to pull focus away from Bella. "We are going to leave early for Calgary tomorrow morning, around 8:00am. We are going to do some shopping before we go to the Calgary Tower and Saddledome."

"Is there a rodeo tomorrow or something?" Charlotte asked.

"You're just going to have to wait and find out," Thom said in a secretive tone. "You're both going to love the Chinook Centre. Over 200 stores."

"That sounds fun. Do we have to shop together?" Charlotte asked.

"No, you can go off on your own. Maybe we'll meet for lunch at some point," Thom suggested.

The girls were excited to shop in new destinations. They were used to the overpriced mark-ups at the Yorkdale Mall and Eaton Centre and the various incense-soaked vintage shops that lined Queen Street. Charlotte and Bella had so many memories of shopping with their mom, and they were always the most delightful times. Thom wasn't a huge fan of shopping but understood how fun it was for the girls.

As they chatted about different stores and new fashion trends, Brody came from the kitchen carrying their food. "Three prime rib dinners. One for you, one for you, and one for you." Brody was very careful and pleasant as he delivered the food. "I hope you enjoy the food," he said as he looked Bella in the eye. "Is there anything else I can get for you?"

"No, thank you." Bella looked back at him. "But maybe in a while."

Brody smiled and made his way to a different table to clear the empty plates of guests.

"You and Brody are going to have babies," Charlotte taunted immaturely.

"Shut up, Charlotte," Bella quipped.

"Both of you be quiet and enjoy the feast that lies in front of you," Thom suggested.

Chapter 6 - Roadtrip

Thom, Bella, and Charlotte hit the road early. The sun was just beginning to peak over the mountains as their rental car made its way onto the main highway into Calgary. Thom showed the girls Mount Rundle as they drove past and were reminded of their first exhausting day in Banff.

"It really does look like a dragon's back," Charlotte said as she looked out the back window in awe.

"That's a really challenging mountain you girls climbed on your first day. You made me super proud," Thom said with his eyes fixed on the road. "People out here have incredibly healthy lifestyles."

As they drove along the two-lane highway, the pristine natural environment of the national park was somewhat overwhelming as the early morning sun illuminated things in a golden light; rivers, ravines, lakes, trees, mountains, and overhangs all seemed like a Monet painting.

Thom squinted at something ahead in the distance. At first, he couldn't make it out, but as it got closer, he realized it was a herd of big-horned sheep crossing the road. The sheep couldn't care less as cars approached. They crossed at their own pace. Thom slowed the vehicle and pulled off on the shoulder of the road.

"Come on girls, let's get a closer look. Grab your cameras," Thom said as he opened his car door.

The girls and Thom got out of the car and slowly crept toward the crossing mountain goats. There was a certain amount of adrenaline involved, as they had never been near wild sheep before.

"They're crossing to graze in that new meadow," Thom said pointing.

"Their horns are huge," Charlotte observed. "They must be heavy."

"30 pounds of horn," Thom said quietly.

They were now within 30 feet of the herd. Both Bella and Charlotte had decent Pentax cameras their father bought for them. They loved taking pictures, getting them developed, and the anticipation of how all the photos turned out. The 35mm Pentax brought a timeless quality to photos. Both girls loved their camera and could never envision life without it.

They snapped several pictures of the herd as they made their way onto the new meadow. They were huge animals, some well over 300 pounds.

"God, they're huge. They're not Mary's little lambs," Charlotte joked.

"Alberta's provincial mammal," Thom said.

The three stood from their crouched positions and watched as the last sheep crossed. It was yet another experience the girls wouldn't soon forget. They made their way back to the car as they looked back to the herd entering the meadow.

"Dad, why aren't they afraid of cars?" Bella asked.

"They're protected animals, so they've never been run over by cars and have never been hunted by humans. Well, at least in the last 100 years. There used to be millions of them until disease, new livestock, and over-hunting nearly wiped them out," Thom explained.

"You sure do know a lot about big-horned sheep, Dad," said Charlotte.

"Maybe a little too much," Bella joked.

The three got into the car and pulled off the shoulder, back onto the main highway, pleased that their morning had begun with such a National Geographic moment. After a few kilometres of highway, they passed a sign for the town of Canmore.

"Do you girls remember the Calgary Olympics in 1988?" asked Thom.

"Kind of. I remember the Olympic glasses you bought at a gas station," Bella said.

"You remember that?" Thom was shocked. "We used to get them at Petro Canada."

"You bought glassware at a gas station?" Charlotte joked.

"Yeah, in hindsight it is kind of strange. In '88, the Olympics were in Calgary and all of the Nordic skiing and biathlons were held in Canmore." Thom felt like a tour guide but enjoyed the role.

"What's a biathlon?" asked Bella.

"It's a long cross-country ski, followed by target shooting, followed by a long ski, crouched shooting, then a long ski, then shooting from lying on your stomach," Thom described.

"That sounds gruelling," Bella said.

"It's supposedly one of the toughest races in the world," Thom said as he raised his eyebrows.

Charlotte thought how neat it would be to ski and shoot for sport. Charlotte sorely missed that athletic side of herself. The shock of her mom passing was devastating for Charlotte's athletic passions. Some of her fondest memories were playing volleyball, baseball, and basketball growing up. Charlotte played for a city championship at age 15 for the senior girls' volleyball team. The crowd energized her that day; all her friends and family were there, including her Mom and Dad. She played the game of her life and took home the championship trophy. She vividly remembers the moment after winning, she looked into the crowd to see her Mom crying with joy, as her Dad wrapped his arms around her. Val was so proud of Charlotte; from the time she was born, all the way to her last moments.

"I'd love to try that," Charlotte said as she shed a tear of joyful remembrance.

"Maybe one day, Char. You'd be so great at it," Thom said.

They finally passed through the Rocky Mountain foothills and into Calgary. Though they were only in the mountains for a few days, they were suddenly reminded of the millions of people in the world. Banff was small and isolated; it felt as if nobody else existed. Calgary was Alberta's largest city with 1.4 million people. It had museums, art galleries, historical villages, a gigantic zoo, malls, a major university, and entertainment for anyone with a pulse.

Their first stop was the Chinook Centre. A huge mall with every store a teenage girl could possibly want. Because it was so early, there was hardly anyone in the mall. As the minutes passed more and more people began to trickle in and the midday sun shone through the skylight windows above.

Bella and Charlotte agreed to meet their dad in 90 minutes at the food court. They were excited to go to every store, even the old lady stores. There were stores with cowboy hats and huge belt buckles, entire stores dedicated to flannel, cowboy boots with all types of designs and, there were the typical stores like the Gap, Bootlegger, and Banana Republic. Bella and Charlotte strolled from storefront to storefront, window to window.

"Are you having fun on the trip so far?" Charlotte asked as they strolled past another store.

"Yes! Are you?" Bella replied.

"It's pretty much the most fun I've had in my life," Charlotte said with a smile.

"Dad seems like he's having fun too. He sure does make friends quick, eh?" Bella snickered.

"I never thought he was that outgoing. But I guess I was wrong," Charlotte said.

"I think we're all starting to come out of our shell a bit. I mean, all three of us lost, pretty much, the most important person in our lives," Bella said as she chucked a penny into a fountain as they passed by.

"Did you make a wish?" Charlotte asked.

"Yes, I did," Bella answered.

"You're not going to tell me, are you?" Charlotte inquired.

"Nope," Bella said sharply.

As the two girls strolled into the Levi Strauss store, two boys in their late teens passed by and smiled at them. Both girls' faces flushed red as they looked at each other and giggled.

Thom loved the bookstore Coles since he first studied Hamlet and MacBeth in high school. The Coles notes helped him to better understand the complex Shakespeare plays as he struggled throughout English class. Thom liked to check out the best sellers list, historical non-fiction books, and whatever he could get his hands on in the field of architecture and engineering.

Today was a little different. He found himself floating to the self-help section of the store. Something he always passed by without any inclination to even look at the works. Thom picked up the book 'Grieving: How to Go on Living when Someone You Love Dies'. He read the back and noticed some key points like: 'how to understand and resolve grief and how to talk to your children.' It felt like he might gain some valuable insight from the book. The book might help guide him through the holidays and other significant days, if anything, it would offer some sort of advice, whether he chose to take it or not. This book was going to help himself as well as his daughters, he thought. He shook his head in affirmation and brought the book to the checkout line.

The girls were browsing the perfumes at The Hudson Bay Company. Though they were not your typical girly-girls, they did have moments where they liked to do each other's hair, put on make-up, and try on fancy dresses. They repeatedly tried different perfumes on their wrists; CK1, Victoria's Secret, Spice Girls Body Spray, Vanilla Fields, Exclamation, and Tommy Girl among others.

The lady behind the counter was more than willing to help as she worked on a commission that earned her more money per sale. It was also still early in the day, so the Hudson Bay store wasn't as busy as it was in the afternoon. The lady offered Sunflowers by Elizabeth Arden and Charlotte recognized the smell right away.

"This is Mom's perfume!" Charlotte said with excitement.

Bella took a whiff of Charlotte's wrist. "Oh, my God, that is Mom."

"It smells like old ladies," Charlotte said laughing.

"Why do you think Mom wore this?" Bella asked.

"Maybe it's what Grandma wore," Charlotte guessed.

"Either way, I don't know what she was thinking," Bella said with a giggle.

"It is very popular amongst our retirement community," the lady behind the counter said.

Bella and Charlotte both looked at each other and laughed.

Thom found himself inside the mall arcade. He loved a good 1990's arcade. Ever since he was a boy, he could always amuse himself with a few quarters. Things began with his pinball addiction in the late 60's but then everything changed when Pong was released in 1972. Thom was still just a boy when the game was released, and he couldn't figure out the engineering magic behind the digital animation. From Pong, his passion morphed toward Space Invaders, Pacman, Donkey Kong, and Centipede.

Thom was still just a kid at heart. He loved adulting from time to time, but he could play video games all night if left to his devices. His new favourite genre was racing games. This particular year, it was Daytona USA; a racing game that put you in the seat of a Nascar driver travelling at speeds over 200 Miles per hour. Games had evolved since Thom was a boy, but his fascination with them never changed.

Thom put a few quarters in the machine and selected his course and car. Three, two, one, go! Thom put his foot to the floor and his car launched into first place. He was in the zone.

"You got nothing. I'm the king. I'm the king!" Thom shouted enthusiastically. "Look out, suckers!"

Bella and Charlotte were sitting and waiting for their father in the food court. Bella was tapping her foot and Charlotte was tapping her fingers. The girls had fun shopping, but they had hit a brick wall. They hadn't eaten in a while and were both feeling tired and lazy after meandering throughout the entire mall.

"Where is dad?" Charlotte slouched, as she put her hand on her cheek.

"He's usually never late," Bella added as her anxiety started to rise.

"I'm hungry," Charlotte whined.

Thom came around the corner and into the sightline of the girls.

"Finally," Bella moaned.

"Sorry girls, I was just taking care of some business stuff," Thom said with a smile.

"What are you talking about?" Charlotte asked indifferently.

"Can we go now?" Bella said coldly.

"It seems you girls might need some food," Thom said. "I'm going to grab some french fries. What do you want?"

"I'm fine. I just want to go," Charlotte said in a testy voice.

"We are not going anywhere until we eat something," Thom said with a manufactured smile.

"French fries, get us french fries," Bella said as she rolled her eyes.

Thom got up and realized exactly what was happening; the same thing had been happening for the past 18 years. He knew the timing and behaviours of the girls when they were hungry. He was also thinking that all this extra physical activity was probably causing their hunger to increase and blood sugar to drop.

Thom ordered three large fries and three toasted bagels with cream cheese. They sat and ate their fries and bagel in almost absolute silence. Thom didn't say much; he knew better than to test the girls until the food kicked in and they started to feel better.

"Guess where we are going next?" Thom asked. There was a pause, and the girls just looked at him as they chewed their food. "We're going to the Calgary Tower. You know the building that looks like the big space needle in Seattle. It has a great view; you're both going to love it."

"Sounds alright," Charlotte said as she wiped her mouth.

"Ok, sounds fine," Bella added as she meticulously organized the trash on her tray.

Thom smiled, as he could see their moods shifting. The three cleared their trays and made their way back through the mall to the parking lot.

They got in the car and made the drive to the Calgary Tower. The trip was a short one, down Macleod Trail and through the heart of downtown. In many ways it reminded Charlotte and Bella of

Toronto, tons of buses, bikes, pedestrians, students, and bustling cafés. They found it almost hypnotic.

The car ride was certainly quiet. The girls were happy to sit in the back seat and nod off as their food digested and they watched midday Calgary. Every few seconds, he would look in his rearview mirror to check on the girls, just as he had been doing for 18 years. It made him smile to see the girls fighting to stay awake as their heads would snap back and forth and let out the occasional snort. Thom remembered turning to Val as they both would quietly laugh together at their girls. Thom and Val knew the easiest way to put the girls to bed was to take them for a car ride on a full stomach.

Thom took his time to admire all the new architecture that was springing up all around Calgary. Condos, railways, plazas, greenspaces, everything seemed so new and clean; quite the opposite of the crowded, old brick architecture in Toronto that was designed during the industrial revolution with the horse and buggy in mind. Traffic seemed to flow better; the sky seemed higher; the air seemed purer as the result of the north westerly winds that made their way from the Arctic.

Thom also noticed the healing that was happening in the girls, as well as his own self; acceptance seemed to be the final stage of the grieving process. Thom was proud of his girls for how far they had come from the first weeks after their mother's passing; the denial, the anger, the sadness, and now the acceptance phase of their healing. The girls were starting to make important decisions that were not determined, or directly influenced, by the loss of their mother.

Thom brought the girls to show them where their parents met, but also, he wanted to show them the vastness of Canada and how many opportunities were laying in front of them. Thom truly believed this was perfect timing for bringing his girls on a life-altering trip; it would be something they would remember for a lifetime. He peeked in the rearview once more and smiled as they both had fallen sound asleep. To Thom, the girls seemed to be able to make their own decisions again, and mature enough to choose wise career paths; something that he thought impossible 18 months ago.

As he passed modern building after modern building, a memory flashed in Thom's mind; a long road trip to Florida when the girls were in elementary school. It was a 17-hour drive to Orlando, and he vividly remembered the sunburnt cheeks, the sandy toes, and the exhausted girls sleeping in the backseat. He smiled as he shed a tear of joy reminiscing about the long day on the sunny shores, making sandcastles, and swimming in the ocean. It was a special trip he would never forget, much like the current western expedition they were on.

Bella and Charlotte woke as Thom pulled into the parking lot of the Calgary Tower. They were both disoriented, but excited to arrive at their destination. Thom was already out of the car stretching his arms over his head.

Bella stepped out of the car. "So cool," she said as she looked up to the massive steel and concrete structure.

"Pretty massive, isn't it?" Thom remarked. "Come on, Charlotte. Let's go. We're waiting for you."

Charlotte was still looking tired in the backseat as she looked out to her sister and father with hazy eyes. She slowly started drifting off and closed her eyes. Bella swiftly banged on the rear window and woke her sister.

"Fine. Fine." Charlotte rolled her eyes and got out of the car. "Let's go," she said with a grumpy tone.

They made their way into the tower, paid the fees, and took the elevator to the top of the structure, the observatory that overlooked the city of Calgary. It was a crystal-clear day with just a few clouds in the sky. The girls, amazed by the view, took several shots with their cameras, and meandered about the 360-degree deck which gave them perspectives of the entire city and distant mountain backdrop.

Thom made his way up behind his girls who were gazing out toward the horizon. "Pretty neat view, isn't it? If you look right out there, you can see the University of Calgary."

Both the girls instantly seemed interested. They both thought how amazing it would be if they both could go to school in Alberta. Toronto and Ontario always seemed certain to be their educational path; they knew that was where their home, family, and friends were. Bella hadn't accepted admission anywhere yet, but instantly felt anxiety about deciding to go to Ryerson, York, or The University of Toronto.

"Maybe we could drive by the campus on the way back into Banff. What do you think?" Thom suggested.

"That would be cool," Bella replied.

"The campus is huge. You'd love it. Plus, there's a couple of new buildings I want to check out," Thom mentioned.

Bella turned and looked at her father. "That sounds great, Dad." She smiled and turned back around to the Alberta landscape with optimistic curiosity.

Charlotte was thinking deeply about Alberta. The mountains, the hiking, the air, the people, Alberta was unlike anything she had ever seen or experienced before. She slowly was beginning to realize Toronto didn't match her energy levels. Moving from box to box, subway to bus, store to store, school to home, didn't appeal to her at all. She had been living it for all her life, but hadn't known anything different, until now. Charlotte was considering, deeply, how her body and mind were feeling; there was a deep-seeded feeling of peace in her soul. The stresses and anxieties she had been feeling could easily be eradicated by exercise, sound sleep, and a healthy diet. Charlotte knew this moment, atop the Calgary Tower, would be a turning point in her life.

After enjoying the views from the Calgary Tower, Thom, Bella, and Charlotte made their way back to the car and onto the main thoroughfare of the city.

"Where are we going next, Dad?" Charlotte asked.

"I got three tickets to the Calgary Stampeders versus the Hamilton Tiger Cats," Thom said excitedly.

"Is that hockey?" guessed Charlotte.

"No, it's football, Char," Thom said with a smile. "I was able to secure some beautiful midfield seats. We're going to be able to kiss Wally Buono."

"Is Wally the mascot?" Charlotte guessed.

"No, he's the coach of Calgary," Thom replied again with a smile. "There's a buzz in this city."

"I hate football," Bella frowned.

"Just you wait," Thom said as he continued to smile. "You're both going to love it."

It took a few minutes to arrive at the football game. They pulled into the gigantic parking lot outside the Saddledome.

"It looks just like a saddle!" Charlotte said as soon as she saw the structure.

There were thousands of people tailgating in the parking lot for opening day. Pretty much everyone was in red Calgary jerseys and various types of cowboy hats and Stampeder attire. Barbeques were smoking, coolers sprawled everywhere, and a mixture of tents and dining shelters were set throughout the lots to shelter the fans from the elements.

Thom crept his way slowly through the parking lot to where he eventually found a spot next to a huge pickup truck. In the bed of the truck sat two large 300-pound, topless men drinking beer in lawn chairs. Charlotte and Bella, both gave them a stink-face as they pulled in.

Thom, Charlotte, and Bella felt out of place. They didn't have jerseys, face paint, propane stoves, or any type of sausage. It was a raucous environment; buffoonery, drunkenness, and indecency were stretched out across five football fields of parked cars and trucks. Granted, it was opening night football in Calgary, but they still couldn't believe the indecency of the mega spectacle and they hadn't even stepped foot inside yet.

They made their way inside the stadium, giving their tickets to the attendant as soon as they entered. There were hot dog stands, beer vendors, apparel shops, 50/50 salesmen, and thousands of Stampeder fans with a few black and gold Hamilton jerseys sprinkled amongst the sea of red and white.

After walking for a few minutes amongst the crowd, Bella did a double take of a boy standing in line at one of the refreshment stands. She couldn't believe her eyes; it was Brody from the lodge in Banff. He was dressed from head to toe in Calgary Stampeder cowboy regalia. She had to say something. She ran up to him and surprised Brody with a shoulder check. He let out a whelp as he stumbled into his dad standing beside him.

"Well, howdy there cowboy!" Bella said with a country twang.

"Jesus, Bella. What the hell are you doing here?!" Brody said, obviously happy and shocked.

"Me and the old man came to see some pigskin," she continued with the country accent.

"Same here. It's so great to run into you. Dad, this is Bella, Charlotte, and their father Mr. Thomas Hudson." Brody introduced his father to everyone as he shook hands with the newfound friends.

"Jim Hughes, nice to meet you," Brody's dad said with a smile.

"Likewise. Ready for a Stampeder stomping?" Thom said.

"This team looks like it's going all the way. What do you think, son?" Jim said as he nudged Brody.

"All-the-way!" Brody said with one hundred percent certainty. "Dad, these folks are staying at the lodge. They've been there a few nights now."

"No kidding? Well, what a coincidence. Where are your seats?" Jim asked.

"Section 30, row D. We're at the 50-yard line," Bella said, as she was looking at her ticket.

Charlotte was just standing there, tapping her foot, and rolling her eyes. "Can we go?" she asked.

"Don't be rude, honey," Thom said. "Why don't you go to your seat and check out the field level?"

"Fine," Charlotte did a 360 and left.

"It's been a long day," Thom chuckled. "Where are you guys sitting?"

"We're in section 30 too, row F. Looks like we're a couple rows behind you. What are the odds?" Jim said.

Brody turned to Bella. "Want to meet up at the end of the first quarter? Top of the stairs?"

"Sure," Bella said casually.

On the inside, Bella couldn't wait for that first quarter to expire; she couldn't care less about football. Though she wasn't used to cowboys, she found herself eerily attracted to Brody's western look. If you dressed as a cowboy in Toronto, people would just laugh at you or think you were filming a movie. On this particular day, Bella's insides were doing cartwheels.

"Say, Thom, maybe at halftime, we could let the kids sit together," Jim suggested.

"Great idea. Let's meet for a beer and hotdog at halftime," Thom responded.

"Perfect. I'll meet you at the top of the stairs," Jim said.

"I'll see you at the end of the first quarter," Bella said.

Thom and Bella made their way down to their seats while Jim and Brody remained in line to grab a pregame snack.

"You little devil," Jim said as he nudged Brody.

The Hamilton Tiger Cats and their quarterback Danny McManus were up 7-0 at the end of the first quarter. Both teams were battling, and the crowd was still in it, cheering at every play and every tackle. As soon as the whistle blew, Bella jumped up and made her way to the top of the stairs where Brody was already waiting. Bella imagined she was the bride, and her groom was waiting for her at the altar. She smiled at the thought.

"Hey!" Brody said when she got to the top.

"Hey!" Bella smiled back.

"Great game, eh?"

"They hit each other so hard," Bella said with a sad face.

"It's a rough game. But we love it. Say, would you want to go for a walk around the stadium?"

"Sure."

The two strolled a while looking at the thousands of people scrambling for the washroom and hotdogs.

"So, do you know what you're doing next year for university?" Brody asked.

"I think I'm going to Ryerson, U of T, or York University. I'm not entirely sure yet," Bella answered. "I want to check out the campuses first."

"If you want to come work at the lodge instead, I'm pretty sure I could get you a job," Brody said jokingly.

Bella laughed, but seriously contemplated not going to school and just working in a beautiful place such as Banff. "Thanks for the offer, that would be so amazing. I've just been dead set on going to university," she said.

"We Albertans put the leisure of living before our careers. If you're not sure what you want to do, there's no sense in going to school and wasting your money," Brody wisely said.

"You're so right. It's been drilled into Charlotte and I's head since we were little that we were going to head to university right after high school, no matter what," Bella said.

"My Mom always says the most interesting people still don't know what they want to do," Brody added. "People out here aren't wrapped too tightly, if you catch my meaning."

"I have some big choices and things to take care of before the end of the summer. I'm just taking my time right now and focussing on making the right decisions. Talking with my grief counsellor, he told all of us not to make any rash impulsive decisions right away. The more time that passes, the better my rationality seems to be working," Bella said as they passed Ralph the Dog, the Stampeder mascot.

Ralph pivoted and grabbed Bella's arm and pulled her into a passionate embrace. She screamed as she was lifted in the air by the mascot's tight grasp. Brody thought it was hilarious. Ralph shook Bella left to right in the air as her legs dangled from side to side. Bella's face began to turn red as more and more people turned to see what the commotion was. Ralph eventually let Bella down to her feet and then proceeded to pet her head like a dog. He then pointed at himself, indicating he wanted to be pet too.

"I think he wants you to pet him," Brody said laughing.

"Bad dog," Bella said as Ralph let out a whimper.

Bella gave him a pet on the head and a scratch behind the ear. Ralph's leg began to shake uncontrollably as the 30 or so onlookers giggled and laughed.

"I think he likes you," Brody joked.

At this point, Bella was beet-red. Brody reached for her hand and tried to pull her away. Ralph pulled back on the other arm and Bella found herself in the middle of a tug-of-war. The crowd continued to laugh as Ralph finally let go. He blew her kisses as he slowly backed away into the crowd.

"What a crazy dog!" Brody said, "That was hilarious."

"Can we leave?" Bella said with a smile. "That was so embarrassing."

Brody took Bella by the hand and led her back through the thousands of fans waiting for nachos and refreshments. She didn't think twice about Brody grabbing her hand; she trusted him; it was something that felt so natural.

The second quarter had started, and Charlotte and Thom were in their seats waiting for Bella to return.

"Do you think they got lost?" Thom suggested.

"I think they're smooching by the nacho stand," Charlotte joked.

Thom laughed then stopped. "Are you serious?"

"Maybe," Charlotte said as she raised her eyebrows.

As the crowd roared for a big defensive tackle by the hometown team, Bella came down the aisle with Brody.

"Sorry, I'm late. We got caught in the washroom lineup," Bella said.

"No problem. I hope you had fun," Thom said.

"Yeah, I hope you had fun," Charlotte said sarcastically.

"Shut your dirty mouth, Charlotte," Bella said viciously.

"So, I talked to Jim, and I'm going to change seats with Brody at halftime. He'll come down here and I'll go up there," Thom announced.

"Great," Bella said with a smile.

The Calgary quarterback pulled off a big run and the crowd went wild.

At halftime the score was 10-0 for Hamilton. Thom popped out of his seat. "I'm going to get a drink. I'll come down and meet you guys after the game. Brody will be down shortly," he said.

"Sounds good, Pop!" Charlotte replied.

"Don't you dare embarrass me when Brody comes down," Bella warned.

"I'm going to tell him the story of when you puked on Mrs. Beamer in grade one," Charlotte said coyly.

"I will smother you with a pillow while you sleep," Bella threatened.

Up at the refreshment stand, Thom met up with Jim who was in line. "Ten-zip Hamilton. Not what I was expecting," Thom said to Jim.

"They're going to come back," Jim said assuredly. "They just got those opening day jitters. The defence looks pretty good."

"Roger that."

"Are you guys going to catch the fireworks at Olympic Plaza after the game?" Jim asked.

"Fireworks? Olympic Plaza? Right, Canada Day. Olympic Plaza, eh? That's a great idea. I didn't even think of going to see fireworks today," Thom said.

"Yeah, I think the kids will appreciate it too. Brody couldn't stop smiling during the second quarter," Jim said with a smile. "I think he may have a little crush on your Bella."

"I haven't seen Bella smile in a while either. Well, not since her Mom passed away," Thom said.

"Your wife passed?" Jim said. "Jesus, I'm sorry to hear that."

"Yeah, about 18 months ago. It's been a rough go for everyone, especially the girls. Going through the process, you know. This trip has been so incredibly good for them, so far," Thom explained.

It was always so hard for Thom to talk about Val casually. She was the love of his life, his best friend, and the mother of his children, and he had so little time to prepare for the inevitable. He was healing and found things easier to talk about, but it would always be tough talking about the emotional rollercoaster that followed her passing. Though Jim was essentially a stranger, he still felt comfortable enough to tell him about Val, after all, he was staying at his lodge and his daughter was hitting it off with his son.

"Jesus, I'm sorry to hear that. Poor girls. Did you get to see a grief counsellor?" Jim asked. "My friend in Drumheller lost her husband on the rigs, and the counsellor really helped her through things. I don't mean to impose; just thought I'd share."

"Yeah, doc was super helpful. He guided us through the roughest times, that's for sure. The anger, frustration, the guilt, the shame, all of it," Thom said as he recalled the darkest, blurriest days in the months following Val's departure.

"Gosh that must have been tough. I'm truly sorry to hear that. I can't even imagine losing Allison and who knows how Brody would take it," Jim said thoughtfully.

"We're on the mend now. Things are going alright," Thom said. "I'm so proud of the girls."

"Say, what are you having? It's on me," Jim offered.

"I'll take whatever you're having, thanks," Thom replied.

"Beer and a dog alright?" Jim asked.

"Perfect," Thom answered.

"Great, let's load up and go watch this Calgary comeback."

Brody made his way down to where Bella and Charlotte were sitting. He waved as he sat down beside Bella, who was in between him and Charlotte.

"Hey!" Brody said. "How's everybody doing?"

"Hi, Brody," Charlotte said in a strange, seductive tone.

Bella turned to Charlotte. "I told you; I will kill you in your sleep," Bella then turned to Brody with a smile. "We're doing great."

"Enjoying the game, so far?" Brody asked.

"Not particularly," Charlotte said.

"We're having a great time," Bella said as she casually stomped the top of Charlotte's foot as she let out a grunt.

It was a back-and-forth game through the third and fourth quarter. Calgary was down 14-20 with two minutes left on the clock. Jeff Garcia and the Stampeders got the ball back and promptly marched down the field. With just under a minute to go, Garcia found his receiver, Travis Moore in the back of the endzone to give Calgary the 21-20 lead. The crowd went berserk as the clock struck zero with Calgary having made the dramatic comeback.

Brody, Bella, and Charlotte were on their feet cheering as loud as they could. Jim and Thom were jumping up and down like little children as they high fived each other and everyone around. It was certainly a great Canada Day for Calgarians as the sun set on the Saddledome.

The five newfound friends met in the mezzanine, all with big smiles on their faces and seemingly out of breath after such an exciting ending to the game.

"Did you see that catch?!" Brody said to his dad as he high fived him.

"Feet down, back of the endzone. Touchdown!" Jim said as he gave the referee signal for touchdown.

"What'd you think, Char?" Thom asked.

"It was okay," Charlotte said as she shrugged.

"She loved it, dad," Bella added.

"So, Mr. Hughes had a great idea. I totally forgot there might be a Canada Day celebration today. So, he suggested we go down to Olympic Square and watch the fireworks. What do you think?" Thom asked.

Bella looked at Brody. "Sounds like fun."

"Fine," Charlotte said as she rolled her eyes.

Jim, Brody, Thom, Bella, and Charlotte made their way to the parking lot among the wave of red jerseys. The city would be much happier tonight because of the Stampeder victory. Fans were blowing horns, whistling, and chanting a variety of slogans as they marched toward the exits. The five friends even joined in a few chants as they walked together with the setting sun in the background.

"So, we'll meet you down there. Do you know where you're going?" Jim asked.

"Yeah, I think so. It's right near the Tower, right?" Thom responded with confidence.

"There's a set of flagpoles there. Maybe that's a good rendezvous," Jim suggested.

"Perfect," Thom said.

"We'll see you down there," Brody said looking at Bella.

"See you," Bella said.

Jim and Brody split from the other three and made their way to their car.

"Bella's got a boyfriend. Bella's got a boyfriend," Charlotte chanted.

"You might too if you weren't such a turd," Bella snapped back.

"I'm prettier than you," Charlotte said with her nose in the air.

"Ok, enough. Pretty funny running into those two, eh?" Thom reflected.

"Crazy," Charlotte said.

Bella couldn't remember being this happy. It had been so long since her body and mind felt at ease. Her physical exhaustion combined with the chemistry shared with Brody planted a seed in her brain. She wanted to feel this good all the time. She didn't want to worry about school, her mom, or missing the bus. It was a true epiphany for Bella; she wanted to feel joy for the rest of her life.

Olympic Square was a bustling place as the sun was fully down and the anticipation of fireworks was almost tangible. A mix of Canadian music was playing on nearby loudspeakers. Kids were screaming and dancing all around with sparklers and glow-sticks that were being sold at various vendors throughout the area. The city was the perfect backdrop; the energy was electric. Buildings were lit up and the moon highlighted the mountains in the background.

Thom and the girls met up with Jim and Brody and all were full of excitement. It truly was the cherry on top of the great day they all had. The signal firework went off indicating the show was about to begin. Charlotte grabbed her dad's arm with excitement. Brody grabbed Bella's hand. It was loud in the square and you could barely hear your own voice with sounds of the music, the children, and crowd.

"Come with me, I know a really cool spot," Brody said into Bella's ear.

She looked at him and then spoke into her dad's ear. "I'll be back, Brody wants to show me a cool spot."

"Sure thing, kiddo. Come back here after they're done. We still have a long drive, and I don't want to wait around," Thom said in a fatherly tone.

Brody and Bella made their way through the crowd as the first fireworks began. They made their way up some steps away from the mob. It was more of a view and gave a clear line of sight towards the display. "What do you think?" Brody asked. "It is a much better view and people don't really know about this spot. I thought you might…"

Just as Brody was about to ramble on, Bella interrupted him. "It's perfect."

Brody turned and looked at Bella as she stared back. She could see the reflections of the fireworks in his eyes. She leaned into him and closed her eyes as they kissed to a soundtrack of cracks and pops of the firework display.

Chapter 7 - The Hot Springs

T hom was up before the girls and made his way down to the dining lounge. He grabbed a newspaper on the way and was eagerly anticipating a nice big cup of strong coffee. He certainly was happy the girls were having such a good time in Banff; his plan was working. Thom knew Bella and Brody were hitting it off and Charlotte was getting back into the groove of being active. He was also thinking about the purchase of a new home in Caledon, just outside of Toronto. Thom knew it was going to be a busy year with having to sell the Toronto home and move into a new residence north of the city, but he wasn't going to let that bother him now. It was going to be another beautiful, busy, active day in Banff.

Thom sat at a table and ordered a coffee and breakfast and looked at the front page of the newspaper which had, yet another picture of Bill Clinton and Monica Lewinsky with the headline that read 'Lewinsky Keeps Silence.'

The ongoing case between President Bill Clinton and Monica Lewinsky had dominated headlines for months and showed no signs of slowing down. There were tapes, juries, perjuries, obstructions, affairs, affidavits, and every other term associated with scandal, affair and/or impeachment. Like many others, Thom just wanted a conclusion to the ongoing scandal, regardless of the outcome.

He flipped the page and began reading an article about the trial. As he was reading and sipping his coffee, Bella showed up alone and sat down beside her dad.

"Hey, kiddo," Thom said with a warm smile.

"Good morning," she replied.

"Did you sleep alright?" Thom asked.

"Like a baby. Charlotte is still sawing logs," Bella joked.

"So is Brody working today?" Thom asked with a coy smile.

"No, he's off today."

"You two are really hitting it off, aren't you?" Thom observed.

"He's cute. He thinks I'm cute. You know," Bella said trying to avoid eye contact and any further conversation related to Brody.

"Yeah, we all had a great time yesterday, but today will be even better, I promise. I have a couple ideas in mind. Tell me if you think they're good. First, we head to the Banff Museum, then over to the Upper Hot Springs, then over to Bow Falls to take in the afternoon scenery; what do you think?" Thom outlined.

"That sounds fun, but I'll need some breakfast first," Bella said.

"So, are you and Charlotte having a good time so far?"

"For sure. We're both realizing how much we need exercise and fresh air in our daily lives," Bella said sensibly.

"It's a lot different out here, isn't it?" asked Thom.

"Everyone is so positive. It makes Ontario seem like a different world."

"Urban environments can sometimes be the loneliest places in the world. People get lazy, they lock themselves up, they walk alone in dark, empty spaces," Thom thoughtfully said. "You have great genes, kid. Your mom and I loved being here together. We loved hiking and never thought we were going to leave."

"Why did you leave Banff?" Bella asked her Dad.

"We both wanted to go to the same university. We got married young; things moved fast when we met."

Bella gave her dad a big smile. She knew the feeling. As Thom's food arrived, Charlotte came into the dining room rocking a colossal messy bun. As she sat down at the table, she grabbed a piece of her dad's bacon and stuffed it in her mouth.

"You look a-dor-a-ble," Bella sarcastically said.

"You couldn't brush your hair?" Thom said.

"I'm hungry," Charlotte said. "And my hair is fine."

"Let's get you girls some food," Thom suggested.

Thom flagged down the waitress with the intent to get Bella and Charlotte food as quickly as possible.

After breakfast, Thom and his daughters made their way on foot to the Banff Museum for the first part of their day's journey. The weather was once again beautiful, not a cloud in the sky. The streets were fairly empty since it was the day after a big holiday.

Bella couldn't stop thinking about Brody and the kiss they shared underneath the fireworks. She was torn between the thought of her getting herself caught up in the moment or truly having feelings for Brody. Afterall, they barely knew each other. Yet, it was an exciting few hours leading up to the fireworks and a wonderful first kiss. Bella knew there was an instant connection between them.

Charlotte, on the other hand, was not as chipper as Bella. Of course, the sisters were close, but when someone came between them, Charlotte had the tendency to go on the defensive, especially if it was a boy. Bella had a boyfriend a while back, and Charlotte made sure she was as cold and distant as possible.

"So, did you feel like Rose on the Titanic last night, Bella?" Charlotte asked without making eye contact.

"Kind of," Bella replied without missing a beat, "Except, my ship definitely isn't sinking."

The Titanic movie had taken the world by storm and quickly became the year's phenomenon. James Cameron was the king of the world and conversations at water coolers everywhere focused on opinions whether there was enough room for both Jack and Rose on the floating door.

"I haven't seen Titanic yet," Thom thought out loud.

"Why haven't you seen it? It's the biggest movie of all time, Dad," Bella said.

Up ahead on the sidewalk, Thom noticed a familiar face. Lacy was in her work attire; a knee-high plaid skirt, a white blouse and her hair tied back in a ponytail. Thom immediately thought of the sexy librarian cliché and couldn't help but put on a big, ridiculous smile as she approached.

"Hi there," Thom said.

"Hey, Thom. Hi Char. Hi Bella. Where are you folks off too?" Lacy asked.

"We're heading to the museum," Thom said.

"I think the Tom Thompson exhibit is still happening," Lacy said.

"So, are we still on for catching a movie on Wednesday? Meet at the Saltlik around 6:00pm?" Thom asked.

"Yes! Tomorrow night. Don't forget. We usually have a blast. Sorry to seem rude, but I've got to catch a board member before 10:00am. I don't mean to rush off," Lacy said.

"No problem, don't let us keep you. I'm looking forward to seeing you tomorrow night. Saltlik 6:00pm," Thom said with a genuine smile.

"Take care. Enjoy the museum," Lacy said.

"Bye," said Charlotte.

"Bye," said Bella.

"See you soon," Thom said.

Lacy walked in the opposite direction from where Thom and his daughters were headed. He instantly felt his heart rate increase and nervous energy course through his body.

"Dad, you're acting like a little kid in a candy store," Bella said observing her dad's energy.

"Daddies got a girlfriend. Daddies got a girlfriend," Charlotte chanted.

"I would never get involved with a woman who lives 3000 miles away. The monthly gas prices would be through the roof," Thom said, thinking he was funny. "Come on, let's go see some old geezer art."

The three of them grabbed the straps on their backpacks and charted their course to The Banff Museum.

Bella, Charlotte, and Thom came out of the museum looking bemused. Looking at oil paintings seems to have that effect on most teenagers and some adults. Thom tried painting once, and realized how much of a perfectionist he was and that he would never be satisfied with his own work. He was baffled that artists like Tom Thomson were able to paint thousands of works in such an impressionist manner and just walk away and move onto the next piece. Thom's obsession came with his architecture background; he couldn't move on unless the colour, value, hue, angle, and perspective were exactly right. He realized art wasn't for him, or at least painting.

"So, what did you think, girls?" asked Thom.

"It wasn't what I expected. Tom Thomson is this famous Canadian artist, member of the Group of Seven and world renown, but his paintings look like a grade one student finger-painted them," Bella said.

"I've wanted to leave since we got here. Let's go to the Hot Springs," Charlotte said.

"You read my mind. It's only a few minutes down the road. Ready to pound the pavement?" Thom asked.

"Yeah!" Both girls screamed at once.

Lacy had arrived back at townhall and was settled back in her office. As much as deadlines, colleagues, and commitments can overtax people, it was almost impossible for Lacy to get stressed or upset. She was too experienced and too wise to allow herself to get pressured. If work piled up; she would just stay late. She loved her job and her co-workers at townhall, especially Barb and Tammy. The three of them shared so much joy and laughter together; they were practically inseparable.

There was a knock at Lacy's door. "Come in," she said, as the door opened on the two smiling faces of Tammy and Barb.

"What is going on sugar buns?" Tammy joked. "Brought you a cappuccino."

"That's great. Just what I need. Hook it to my veins," Lacy said in a Frankenstein voice.

"Can we sit or are you swamped?" Barb asked.

"Sit down. I need a break anyway," Lacy said as her friends sat down.

"So, Deep Impact is sold out tomorrow night at the theatre and the only movie is Titanic," Barb said with a sad face.

"I could see that again," Lacy said.

"It is a pretty fantastic movie," Tammy added.

"Well, I'm okay with it, if you're okay with it," Barb said.

"I hope Thom is okay with it. He's probably already seen it two or three times by now," Lacy said.

"I don't think he will give a flying french fry, as long as he's sitting beside you," Tammy nudged Barb next to her.

"I just want to see the people fall off the end of the boat again and watch them smack the propellers on the way down," Barb laughed.

"You're morbid," Tammy said laughing. "I want to see Jack and Rose have the spitting contest again."

"Gross. I want to see the old lady drop the necklace in the sea," Barb said.

"Weird," Tammy said. "I want to see that Billy Zane in a tux again."

"Strange," Barb rebounded. "I want to see the 'Unsinkable' Molly Brown annoy everyone at dinner again."

"Okay, okay, we'll go see it again," Lacy said. "Will you two be able to sit there for another 3 hours without disturbing anyone?"

"Can't promise anything," Barb answered.

"I'm gonna plead the fifth on that one," Tammy followed as all three of them shared a good laugh.

Thom, Bella, and Charlotte arrived at the Upper Hot Springs with great anticipation. There were only about a dozen or so cars in the parking lot, which was a good sign it wasn't going to be too busy. The Springs were surrounded by pine and spruce trees which combined with the hot steam to welcome each visitor with a pleasant aroma.

The building was a two-story lodge-style structure which blended in with most buildings in Banff. Inside were the changerooms, staffroom, and payment office with a few scattered employees. Thom paid for him and the girls and they made their way into separate change rooms. Both change rooms were virtually empty, so all three got changed quickly and jumped into the showers to rinse off before heading out onto the pool deck.

The large pool was shaped like a 50-foot snowman that overlooked the side of Mt. Rundle. The pool deck was made of stone and the short walls were made of brick and mortar. About 20 or so people occupied various corners of the pool, most of whom were leaning back with their eyes closed. Steam was pouring off the water's surface as the result of being heated from two miles below the earth's surface.

Thom got in first, walking slowly down one of the pool's eight ladders. It was hot, nearly 110 degrees. It took some getting used to, but Thom finally settled in. He beckoned his girls to come in. Charlotte dipped her foot in to test it and jumped back from the heat of the water. She then made her way to one of the ladders and slid down into the pool. "Hot, hot, hot," she said as her shoulders went under.

Bella couldn't accept that Charlotte was brave enough and she wasn't. She didn't even test the water. She delicately slid down the ladder and splashed Charlotte in the face. "No problem, no problem," Bella said, trying to catch her breath. "Frigging hot."

The three of them each found a nice quiet spot along the edge of the pool and found full relaxation. Tranquil music was playing to help soothe the guests and uplift their experience. A cool mountain breeze also helped to regulate everyone's temperature; too cool, submerge, too hot, emerge. After some long hikes and even more walking, it was nice for Thom, Bella, and Charlotte to go through such a therapeutic, healing experience together.

The peace was shattered by three teenage boys who seemingly had no volume control on their voices. They came barging through the doors talking about 'sick trails,' 'full gainers', 'backsides' and 'corkscrews'. The three boys threw their towels on the fence and jumped in, totally disregarding the serene state of everyone around them.

"Send it!" one of them yelled as they jumped in.

"Full send!" another said.

Charlotte couldn't help but be a little curious. The boys looked about her age. Bella couldn't have cared less and found herself disgusted as the rambunctious boys continued to horse around.

"God, could they be any more annoying?" Bella stated.

"I think it's kind of cute," Charlotte replied.

"You make me sick."

"They're just trying to have a good time."

"While totally disregarding everyone else?" Bella rebounded.

The three boys began getting on each other's shoulders and jumping in the water. You could see every bather's eyes rolling as they continued to hoot and holler. Charlotte watched them having fun and wished she could have joined in.

Charlotte had never had a serious boyfriend. Her coming of age coincided with the passing of her mother and had troubles talking to boys. Though she was an outgoing young girl, she would get extremely nervous talking to boys. She had kissed boys before, but nothing serious. None of her past experiences ignited her adventurous, extroverted spirit.

One of the boys in the pool was particularly cute; he had long, blonde wavy hair. He was the most reserved among the boys. He wasn't the one causing the terrible ruckus.

Charlotte and the blonde boy made eye contact after he emerged from underwater and the two seemed to have an immediate connection. Charlotte gave him a little smile as she leaned on the side of the pool. The boy's face became an even deeper shade of red as seemed shocked to see a pretty girl smiling at him. He gave her an awkward smile and tried to play it as cool as possible.

The boys eventually calmed down and leaned against the pool walls about 20 feet from Charlotte, Bella, and Thom.

"You are such a dirty flirt," Bella whispered to Charlotte.

"Stop," Charlotte said as she brushed her hair back like a shampoo commercial model.

"Why don't you say hello?" Bella asked.

"What are you girls whispering about?" Thom interrupted.

"Girl stuff, Dad," Bella responded and turned back to Charlotte. "You know how shy boys can get around girls. Sometimes, girls have to make the first move."

"What should I say?" Charlotte asked.

"He does have cool hair," Bella suggested.

The blonde boy couldn't stop staring across the pool at Charlotte. She took a deep breath and walked across the shallow pool to the ladder.

"Hey," the boy in the polka dot trunks said.

"Hey. I like your swim trunks," Charlotte immediately regretted her comment.

"Thanks," he said with a smile.

Charlotte got out of the pool and grabbed her towel, which was all a ruse to pass by the boy. She snapped her bikini bottoms in the direction of the boy and made her way into the changeroom. The boy couldn't take his eyes off her as she walked away, which Bella couldn't help but notice and laugh a little.

"I think Char is trying to flirt," Bella said to her dad.

"Hmm?" Thom grunted as deep relaxation had kicked in and very little could bother him.

The boy hopped out of the water and started drying off as Charlotte re-emerged from the changeroom.

"Hi, I'm Zach. It's nice to meet you."

"I'm Charlotte. Nice to meet you too."

"Are you here on vacation?" Zach asked.

"Yeah, me, my sister and my dad are here for another week or so."

"Cool. My friends and I are about to start backpacking across the Rocky Mountains this summer."

"So cool," Charlotte said. "What's first?"

"I think we're heading to Jasper first, then wherever the wind takes us," Zach said. There was a short pause while they maintained eye contact. "There's a pretty sweet punk band playing at the Rose and Crown tomorrow night, if you're interested. Maybe your sister can come along too. It's all ages, so you don't need to worry about ID."

"That could be fun. What time does the show start?" Charlotte asked.

"8:00pm," Zach quickly responded.

"That could be really fun. I'll ask her and maybe we'll come along."

"Radical," Zach said as he gave the shaka, the friendly surf sign for 'hang loose.'

"Hopefully, we'll see you later on. Bye Zach," Charlotte said smiling.

"Bye Charlotte," Zach smiled back.

Charlotte threw her towel down and slid back into the water. She swam back over to Bella with a big smile on her face. Bella couldn't help but feel a little joy for her baby sister. She knew these past couple of years had been difficult and there was very little jubilation in their lives. Though it was a small victory, it still felt monumental to see her sister gleefully float toward her.

"What was that all about?" Bella immediately asked as Charlotte returned.

"I'll tell you later," Charlotte said as she leaned back and closed her eyes.

Brody was chopping a variety of vegetables in the lodge kitchen in preparation for the evening's dinner service. His dad was close by boiling a few different sauces. Both Brody and Jim were passionate about cooking and hospitality. They loved feeding and nourishing people and bringing smiles to their faces.

"Brody, I need a box of penne from dry storage," Jim said to his son.

"Roger, big whisky," Brody dropped his knife and made his way into the hallway.

"Grab two cans of tomato sauce too," Jim added.

"Ten four, big dog," Brody said.

As Brody was leaving, his mother, Allison, came into the kitchen. She was dressed in a nice formal skirt and blouse with a name tag that read 'Allison'.

"We just got a reservation for 12 at 6:00pm," Allison said to her husband.

"Great. We are almost ready for service," Jim said, stirring the various pots.

"What's the dessert special tonight?" Allison asked.

"I've got a few lemon meringue and key lime pies cooling in the walk-in," Jim proudly said.

"Mmm, my favourite," Allison leaned in and kissed Jim on his sweaty cheek. "You're the best."

"Thanks honey pumpkin," Jim said as he peeked at the roasting potatoes in the oven.

"I'm going to set up table 40 and 41 together for the reservation," Allison said.

"Great idea. What's the occasion for them?" Jim asked.

"It's an 80th birthday party," Allison answered as Brody came back into the kitchen carrying a box with two large cans of tomato sauce on top."

"Hi, honey bunches," Allison said to her son. "It's going to be a busy night."

"Great, busy nights go way faster," Brody said as he picked up his knife and continued to chop the raw vegetables. "Mom, remember I need tomorrow night off."

"Right, I almost forgot. Thanks for reminding me," Allison said as she left the kitchen.

"Alright, let's get that soup reduced, Brody boy," Jim said in an ultra-positive voice.

Thom, Charlotte, and Bella made their way onto the path that led to Bow Falls. All three of them were feeling relaxed and reborn after a couple of hours at the Upper Hot Springs. Charlotte was feeling especially great after her flirtatious endeavour with the blond-haired boy, Zach.

The route was relatively flat terrain that weaved its way through the evergreen forest. The path had been worn down by the thousands of visitors that had ventured there to catch a glimpse of the epic falls.

The start of the Bow River began in the Rockies, from melting ice and snow from the mountain tops; it then wove through Banff, into Calgary, sprawled into the prairie flatlands and eventually ended at Hudson Bay. In Banff, the Bow River waters were frigid and a great place to take a polar plunge if you were feeling brave enough.

Thom, Charlotte, and Bella were enjoying the simple hike as the sun shone through the trees and with the sound of the river provided peace. Thom pointed out the towering Banff Springs Hotel. The girls were stunned at the size and grandeur of the 19th century stone structure. Thom went on about the Grand Railway Hotels, the Canadian Pacific Railway, and architects Walter S. Painter and Bruce Price. He spoke to the girls of the great influence they had on both him and other famous architects; the girls were only mildly interested.

Throughout the past few days, Charlotte and Bella were used to seeing spectacular things and Bow Falls was no exception. Both were conditioned to only seeing streets, concrete, and skyscrapers that masked any type of pristine nature around them. Bella and Charlotte contemplated their ancient ancestors, the Indigenous people who had navigated this river for so long and what it would have been like 10,000 years ago. They pondered the canoes that would have travelled this river, the people who would have drunk from the river's edge, and the various industries that would have needed the power of the river to support the progress of the times.

Both girls felt lost in time; they both could have been explorers in centuries past, or prospectors looking for gold; they could have been early scientists, like Mary Walcott, measuring and observing the wonders of the glaciers in the Rocky Mountains. Their imaginations were running wild as their hearts were pumping, their feet were moving, and their minds were creating.

Thom had been noticing almost immediate changes, in both himself and the girls. Their demeanours were changing. They weren't as snappy, or as negative as a few weeks earlier. They were funnier, they were kinder, and they were much more charming in the company of others. Thom was very aware of how living in the 'big smoke' came with breathing toxic, industrial air, it felt constantly constrained, often generating great burdens of loneliness, anxiety, and depression. However, Banff felt just like it did when he first met Valerie. It felt like the perfect sized community, where they had everything they needed without the burdens of traffic, inflation, terrible drinking water, or masses of populations that wanted nothing to do with you.

The three family members came upon Bow Falls as if it was some magical gateway to a utopian paradise. The roar of the rapids was loud providing a vibration within their body and soul. From the path, they made their way to the observation deck that had a few benches sprawled along the wooden deck. Bella, Charlotte, and Thom all chose to sit by themselves on separate benches to take in the scene and do some quiet contemplation.

Charlotte opened her water bottle and took a long drink as she thought about what might happen tomorrow night when she and Zach would meet up. What would she say? What would she wear? Would he kiss her? What time is too late to stay out? She took several deep breaths as she felt the euphoria of anticipating the social engagement to come.

Bella, at the same time, was thinking about the kiss she and Brody shared beneath the stars and fireworks. She was also feeling a great sense of pride for her sister who struggled finding connections with boys and was finally able to gain some confidence. She would do anything for her sister. Tomorrow night, she would be with her every step of the way to make sure everything went smoothly. Bella was also thinking about her father from a new perspective. For most of her life, he was the father figure; the disciplinarian, a jerk at times, and almost inhuman for not letting her do all the things that she wanted. Yet, she was starting to see the vulnerable side and the sadness that must have enveloped him since the passing of her mother and his wife. She saw his sensitivity, his kindness, and his dedication to raising his two daughters in the best way he could. Bella loved her father, but never truly humanized him until now.

Thom admired the falls as he once did with Valerie, decades ago. On that day, he and Val sat upon the same bench and shared stories of their youth and upbringing together. He wanted to feel that same warmth and tenderness again. Banff reminded him of how great he felt in the outdoors and how much more exercise he was getting at higher altitudes. His lungs were expanding, his waist was slimming, and his mind was clearing as the days went by.

After an hour of mindful relaxation at the side of Bow Falls, Thom, Bella, and Charlotte made their way back into town. It was a quiet walk back, as the three of them didn't feel the need to create any type of small talk. It had always been difficult for Charlotte and Bella not to feel the need to talk, as they were young girls, but now they felt a safe, secure sense of belonging where silences didn't need to be filled in with conversation just for the sake of it. Their internal conversations were becoming more profound with each day that passed. Thom certainly was becoming more aware of their growth and their journeys to becoming enlightened, individualistic women.

Back at the lodge kitchen, Jim and Brody were hard at work. Now there were multiple cooks and dishwashers scrambling about and doing various tasks within the organized chaos.

Jim called out to the chefs surrounding him: "Two ribeye's, both medium rare, both with mashed and green beans. One with no gravy!"

Mark, the chef manning the grill yelled, "Yes, chef!"

Servers came in and out of the kitchen, always with their hands full. Racks of glasses, plates, pots, and silverware were lined up ready for washing. The two dishwashers had dirty dishes stacked everywhere and were visibly soaked from the splashback in the sink. Although it was pure chaos, Jim managed to keep his cool.

Jim enjoyed the dinner rush; it was like skydiving or bungee jumping for him. The adrenaline he got from feeding 200 people in a couple of hours was exhilarating. "New order: three chicken alfredo's and one gourmet burger with fries!" he yelled out.

"Yes, chef!" Mark yelled again.

"Yes, chef!" Suzy, the pan chef yelled.

Allison came into the kitchen in her managerial outfit. "Chef, may I?" she asked.

"Go ahead," Jim smiled at her.

"The reservation is here. Menus are in their hands, and I just poured their waters," Allison said to her husband.

"Thank you," Jim said in his best professional voice. "I need all hands-on-deck. Party of twelve is about to order," he announced to the kitchen staff.

"Yes, chef!" everyone yelled.

Allison went back into the dining room as Brody came into the kitchen carrying an arm full of dirty plates. "Table 35 loves the penne, chef! Perfect spice!" Brody yelled across the line to working chefs.

"Excellent!" Suzy shouted.

Brody dropped his load of dirty dishes to Sammy and Ben, the two disgruntled dishwashers who were, literally, in over their heads among the dishes. "Can I get you boys a drink?" Brody kindly asked the boys.

"Sure, I'll have a Coke," Sammy said.

"Sprite, please," Ben said.

Brody went back into the dining room and grabbed an empty drink tray as he went. The dining room was packed; not an empty table to be seen. Brody made his way around the tables and picked up various empty glasses. Once his tray was full, he made his way to the bar where he unloaded the empty glasses by the turnstile dishwasher. He then asked Maggie, the bartender, for Ben and Sammy's soda and waited until she poured. As she was pouring, Bella, Charlotte, and Thom came in and waited at the hostess stand, where Allison was going over her reservation book.

Brody was taken aback by Bella, once again. He just watched her for 20 or 25 seconds until he caught her eye. They both immediately smiled at one another, and each felt an endorphin rush through their bodies.

Allison led Thom, Charlotte, and Bella to the only empty table in the restaurant, which was right next to the party of twelve's table. At the head of the party-table was a grumpy looking man with a terrible haunch on his shoulders from years of crotchety opinions and disgruntled viewpoints. Clearly, the man either didn't like celebrating his birthday or he just didn't like crowds and had no desire to be there.

Thom and the girls sat down feeling great. They had hiked, soaked in hot springs, gained educational knowledge throughout the day, and were now fresh out of the shower, in clean clothes, and ready for a delicious meal.

"We have a wonderful chicken alfredo a la penne special this evening, along with a gourmet Italian minestrone," Allison said as she handed out menus to Thom and the girls.

"That sounds terrific," Thom said smiling. "You're making my mouth water."

Brody noticed his mother sat Thom and his girls in his section and would be taking care of them this evening. He was nervous, but excited for the opportunity to be close to Bella, her sister, and father. He didn't want to seem too excited, so he got the dishwasher's sodas and went back into the kitchen to drop them off.

There was a great juxtaposition between the calm, warm, low-lit dining room, and the frantic, loud, hot, and bright kitchen. Jim, Suzy, and Mark were frantically cooking dozens of dishes. There were at least 20 cuts of meat on the grill, a half dozen pans were sizzling, and the fryers were going full blast. Ben and Sammy in the dish area were also busy as could be. Ben scrubbing, and Sammy pulling racks in and out of the dishwasher as his glasses fogged each time the door opened.

"Ben, Sammy, here you go," Brody said as he handed the sodas over the mountain of dishes.

"Thanks, boss," Ben said.

"Thanks, Brody," Sammy said gratefully.

"No problem," Brody said as he turned to go back in the dining room and make his way to Bella's table.

Thom, Bella, and Charlotte were all looking at their menus, but they already knew what they wanted.

"So, are you thinking what I'm thinking?" Thom asked the girls.

"Minestrone to start and chicken alfredo as the main?" Bella replied.

"That's what I want too," Charlotte added.

Thom shut his menu. "Perfect. Me three."

Brody arrived at the table. "Hello, Mr. Hudson. Hi Bella. Hi Charlotte. How's everybody doing this evening?"

"Doing great, Brody. Thanks for asking," Thom said.

"We have a lovely Italian minestrone soup this evening along with a beautiful chicken alfredo. My mom might have told you about it already."

"That was your mom?" Bella asked.

"Yeah, it's definitely a family business around here," Brody chuckled.

"She's so pretty," Bella said.

"Maybe I'll bring her over after your meal and I'll introduce everyone," Brody suggested.

"Great idea," Bella added.

"That would be fine," Charlotte said somewhat regally and sarcastically.

"Sounds terrific, Brody," Thom said giving Charlotte a cross look. "I think we are ready to order; we are starving. To make it simple, I think we're having three minestrones to start and three alfredos for the entree."

"Wonderful!" Brody said while writing it down, though he didn't really need to; he just liked looking the part. "And what would you like to drink?"

"Shall we get a bottle of wine?" Charlotte asked in a dignified manner.

Thom laughed. "Funny! Maybe another time, precious. I'll have a coke."

"Coke for me," Bella said smiling.

"Me too," Charlotte said as she slouched in her chair.

"Terrific. I'll be right back with your drinks," Brody smiled at Bella and walked away.

"Sit up, dear. You know slouching isn't good for you," Thom said.

"So, Dad, me and Bella got invited to a show tomorrow night by that boy at the hot springs," Charlotte casually said.

"Is that so? What kind of show?" Thom had an inkling of what was happening. There were only two places to see bands in Banff and he knew of them quite well. So, he played dumb.

"It is a show, like with dancing and singing," Charlotte said.

"Oh, it must be at a theatre then?" Thom asked.

"It's at the Rose and Crown theatre. It's an all-ages show," Bella said.

"Isn't the Rose and Crown a bar?" Thom wondered aloud.

"I don't know. The boy from the hot springs said it was a place, he never mentioned what it was," Charlotte said in her most innocent voice.

"Well, you can both go if there is no boozing or sleepovers. I want you back at the lodge by midnight. Is that fair?" asked Thom.

"Perfectly!" Charlotte was excited. She turned to Bella. "Hey, maybe Brody wants to go."

"I'll ask him," Bella said.

One of the younger women at the old man's birthday party put a large gift in front of the sour-looking man. "Happy birthday!" she said as the old man refused to look the gift horse in the eyes.

The old man, with no urgency at all, began to unwrap the gift revealing a colourful gift basket. He revealed each item, one at a time. The basket held Pepto Bismol, denture cleaner, Preparation H, a weekly pill calendar, Tums, Bengay, Advil, emergency underpants, a mug that read 'Grumpy Old Man', Memory Mints (for the senior moments) and a novelty 'Weener Kleener' soap ring. Everyone at the table found it ridiculously hilarious; all except the poor old man who was at the brunt of the joke-gift.

"You make me feel so loved and important," The old man said sarcastically.

Charlotte turned to her father. "Just think Dad, that could be you someday," she teased.

"Did he just say 'Weener Kleener'?" Thom laughed.

There was great energy in the room. People were genuinely happy and grateful to be at the lodge, including Bella, Charlotte, and Thom. It had been a while since they wanted to be in the present, surrounded by people, opposed to making excuses and staying secluded. Thom enjoyed this; it was his intention all along.

Thom, a few months before went into Bella and Charlotte's school for parent/teacher night and had the opportunity to speak to all their teachers. He got a lot of the same comments: 'she hasn't been applying herself', 'she has been missing a lot of class', 'I worry about approaching her', and 'her academics have dropped off'. He sometimes wondered if the teachers knew or even cared that Charlotte and Bella had lost their mother.

Thom obviously knew the reason for their failings, and was doing his best, under the circumstances, to help his girls heal from the trauma of losing their primary caregiver. This vacation, so far, was very telling of what Bella and Charlotte needed most in their lives. Everything was coming into focus for Thom.

Brody brought the drinks and a basket of rolls with some small packages of butter to the table. Soon after, he brought the minestrone soups which were devoured in almost complete silence. It had been a long day and they were certainly hungry. The soup suspended their hunger while they waited for the homemade chicken alfredo Jim and his staff were preparing.

"So, how are you girls enjoying Banff and Alberta so far? Tell me honestly," Thom casually asked.

"I love it," Charlotte immediately said, without hesitation.

"It seems like a totally different country," Bella reflected. "People in Toronto act like they're the centre of the world and they understand what is happening throughout the country, when they actually have no idea how different it is out here."

"You're very right, Bella." Thom smiled.

"This country is huge, there's so much going on and so many people," Bella added.

"It kind of feels like something out of a Disney movie," Charlotte said in a supportive manner.

"Banff is like a huge playground and people here prioritize play," Thom said. "Generations and generations have admired this place for thousands of years and it's up to us to keep it this way."

Brody came carrying three plates of chicken alfredo and dropped them off to the table. "Would you care for some fresh parmesan cheese?" he asked.

"Yes, please!" Thom said affirmatively.

"No thanks," Bella said with a smile.

"Is that the armpit cheese?" Charlotte asked.

"Yes," Bella said as she snickered.

"No, thank you," Charlotte immediately said.

Brody grated the cheese onto Thom's penne. "Can I get you anything else?" he asked.

"I think we're good," Thom said.

Brody smiled and walked back into the kitchen.

"Bon appétit," Thom said as the three began to devour their meals. Just as they began their meal, Brody, Allison, Maggie, and a couple of other staff members came out carrying a birthday cake and singing 'Happy Birthday' to the old man sitting behind them.

Though he was grumpy all meal long, this seemed to bring him back to his childhood. He stared with a wide-eyed gaze at the dozens of candles atop the brilliant cake. He let loose his first smile of the evening as he looked from family member to family member. Everyone clapped once the song was over as he struggled to blow out the candles.

It was a joyous scene. Thom smiled at his daughters. "I hope that is me one day," he said.

"Thank you everyone for coming," The old man said to his family as a tear rolled down his cheek. "I love you all."

Charlotte was the first to finish her alfredo, followed by Bella and Thom.

"That was gosh darn delightful," Charlotte said.

"So good!" Bella added.

"I don't think I've ever had pasta that tasted so good," Thom said.

Brody came and cleared the plates. The old man's birthday party eventually left, and the dining room was thinning out after a busy night. Allison came to the table carrying three slices of fresh lemon meringue pie. "Compliments of the house," she said as she delivered them to Bella, Charlotte, and Thom.

"Wow, amazing," Thom said. "You shouldn't have."

"Thanks a bunch, Mrs. Hughes," Bella said with a smile.

"It's no problem at all. You must be Bella. Brody has told me a lot about you," Allison said while setting out napkins and forks.

"I am," Bella responded.

"He told me you had a great Canada Day together at the football game and watched fireworks," Allison said.

Brody came to the table and stood next to his mother. "Hi, mom. This is Bella, Charlotte, and Thom."

"Quite a coincidence you meeting each other at the game," Allison said.

"Funny how small this world can be sometimes," Thom said to Allison.

"Truly," she responded. "I hope you've had a great night. Enjoy your homemade pie."

"Thanks, Mrs. Hughes," Charlotte said.

"Thanks again," Brody said to his mom as she walked back into the kitchen.

"This meal has been wonderful," Thom said to Brody. "And the service has been excellent."

"I'm so stuffed," Charlotte said.

"Say, Brody, do you want to go to the Rose and Crown tomorrow night with me and Char?" Bella asked.

"That sounds great," Brody replied. "I heard about that show. Want to maybe meet in the lobby around 7:30pm?"

"Perfect!" Bella said. "Charlotte is going to come too. She's meeting up with some people there."

"I can't wait," Brody said as he topped up their water glasses.

After the delicious homemade pie, Thom, Bella, and Charlotte went to their room and fell asleep almost immediately.

Later, after all the customers left the restaurant, Brody, Allison, Jim, Maggie, Suzy, Mark, Sammy, and Ben all sat down at the end of the night and had a celebratory sit down which included a few beers, some left over alfredo and a few pieces of key lime pie. Jim and Allison loved their staff and rewarded them for all their hard work and diligence; tonight, was no exception.

"I just want to thank everyone for a great night," said Jim. "You people never cease to amaze me."

"Cheers!" said Allison as she raised her glass. "To the best team in the world."

Everyone said 'cheers' and clinked their glasses.

Chapter 8 - Date Night

Lacy slowly opened her eyes to early morning sunshine. She had a house up on Jasper Way, a street with an immaculate view of Mount Rundle, the mountain that Thom, Charlotte, and Bella climbed on their first day in Banff. Lacy's room was bright and she seldomly needed the reminder from her alarm clock to get up. She put on a housecoat and made her way downstairs to make her first cup of coffee of the day. Beside the kitchen, Lacy had converted the dining room into her personal drafting area, now covered with various blueprints and other projects. There were models of houses, buildings, parks, and commercial buildings; some big, some small.

Lacy filled the coffee maker with water, scooped in the coffee, and flipped the switch to start the pour. She walked on to her porch to find the Calgary Herald on her doorstep. Her house was a duplex and her neighbour, Bob, was on the porch getting ready to take his golden retriever, Hank, for a walk.

"Hi-ya," Bob said.

"Good morning," Lacy said.

"Heading into work today?" Bob asked.

"Yeah, I just need some caffeine first," Lacy joked as she sipped her coffee.

"Supposed to be another beautiful day. Hank is excited," Bob said as he got up patting Hank's side.

"Have a nice day. Bye Hank," Lacy said as Hank gave a friendly bark.

Lacy grabbed her morning paper and read the headline: 'Clinton Facing Possible Impeachment'. She then went inside to finish her coffee and grab a quick bite before heading off to work.

Outside the lodge, Thom, Charlotte, and Bella were dressed for a casual day on the town. Bella and Charlotte were heading off on their own to do some shopping. Thom had a few business calls to make back in Toronto. They said their goodbyes and went off in different directions.

Bella and Charlotte were looking forward to checking out the small little village and all the different little shops it had to offer. The town was full of shopping diversity. Their first stop of the day was at a cute little boutique tea shop. The girls loved tea in the morning just like their mom did. Charlotte ordered a peach tea, and Bella ordered a raspberry tea.

"I slept so great last night," Charlotte said as they both waited for their tea to be served.

"Same," Bella responded.

"Maybe it's the fresh air and exercise. But I close my eyes and as soon as I open them it's morning," Charlotte reflected. "I'm not having any bad dreams either."

"Right?" Bella added.

The young lady behind the counter served them their teas and they stepped outside into the sunshine. Across the street, the same Indigenous woman that Thom purchased the dream weavers from, looked up to the girls coming out of the tea shop and smiled.

Charlotte and Bella marched on until they got to the Banff Shopping Centre, which was full of clothing shops and outdoor wear boutiques. Of course, Bella and Charlotte had clothes with them, but they wanted to buy a special outfit for tonight at the Rose and Crown. They had no idea what they were looking for, but they would know it when they saw it.

The first store the girls went into was a ski and snowboarding shop. It had everything to do with winter sports. A huge retail space with one-piece suits, jackets, snow-pants, toques, goggles, shoes, skis, ski wax, snowboards, and all the brand name t-shirts and casual wear for hip mountain adventurers. Billabong, Columbia, Burton and Quiksilver products dotted the entire store. Bella and Charlotte split up and began looking around.

Charlotte loved the style of snowboarders. Baggy pants, flannel tops, hoodies, and skate shoes were the style and she embraced it. The whole store reminded her of Zach, the boy from the hot springs. She really had no idea what to wear, and she didn't really care much. Bella knew exactly what look she was going for tonight. She was looking for a cute top, lavender, possibly purple, khaki pants, and a long sleeve flannel that would tie easily around her waist if it got too hot. Her hair would be in pigtails, and she would need some lipstick to match her top.

The staff in the store were so tragically hip it hurt; young, laidback, well-dressed, and drinking exotic beverages. Though they didn't find anything, the girls loved the store and cordially said goodbye to the clerks and made their way to the next store.

The next store they entered was a western outfitters store complete with cowboy hats, flannel shirts, belts, buckles, bolos, sheepskin coats, blankets, and all types of Wranglers.

"We have to try some things on," Charlotte said.

"I'll grab you some outfits to try on," Bella said as she smiled and looked around.

"I'll do the same for you. Yee-haw. Giddy up cowgirl," Charlotte said back.

The girls wandered about and got some ridiculous outfits. They found ponchos, western shirts, chaps, cowboy hats of all sorts, leather jackets, western suede fringe, and loads of denim. The girls spent the next half hour or so trying on each individual outfit, then bursting out into laughter when they revealed themselves. Each combination gave them particular walking styles and gestures that reflected each individual outfit.

The store clerk, a 60-or-so year-old man, heard all the laughter and finally got up enough energy to get up off his stool and see what the commotion was.

"Do you girls need any help with anything?" the old clerk asked.

"No thanks," the girls said at the same time behind the change room doors.

"Let me know if there's anything I can do for you," the clerk said as he walked back to the counter where his magazine lay.

After having fun trying on cowboy outfits, they put everything back and made their way outside.

"We could not quite find what we were looking for," Bella said to the old clerk.

"No problem. Have a nice day," he said without raising his eyes from the article he was reading.

Once they were outside, they each gave a giggle and kept walking down the street.

"I want to do that again," Charlotte said laughing.

Thom sat at the cafe where he met Lacy. He was having a coffee and bagel while reading the newspaper. It was hard this day to focus on the article he was reading. There was a lot on his mind. He needed to call his real estate agent about the deal on the house in Caledon and speak with him about selling the Toronto home. Thom knew the girls were going to have a tough time with the transition, but he knew it was the best thing for everyone. He also had to make a call into the firm in Toronto about upcoming projects, evaluations, proposals, deadlines, and other commitments. He knew it was going to be a busy year.

Thom finished his bagel, folded up his newspaper, and pulled out his datebook and Nokia cell phone. He dialled his real estate agent's number and got an answer right away. "Chris, it's Thom Hudson…How are things?"

"Thom, great to hear from you. How was your Canada Day?" Chris said with a slightly staticky voice.

"Fine, fine. Me and my girls went to Calgary for the Stampeders game," Thom replied.

"That sounds like a blast. Hey, listen, I'm gonna be straight up honest with you. I just got some bad news regarding the Caledon house," Chris said in his most earnest voice.

"What's the issue?" Thom asked.

"Well, I've been trying to get a hold of you. There must be some reception issues in the mountains, or something. But the mortgage approval from your bank did not go through, mainly because you're a single income now and things got a bit more complicated. I wanted to arrange a new financing plan, but I couldn't touch base. Also, the sellers were in a bit of a pinch and wanted to sell quickly so they went with different buyers," Chris said painfully.

"Dammit!" Thom yelled, as everyone in the cafe turned to look at him. He covered the phone and said: "Sorry, everyone." He went back to his phone conversation. "Chris, did they close already with the other buyers? Can we put in another offer? I'm sure I can refinance quickly."

"I'm afraid not," Chris said remorsefully. "Maybe a few days ago, but not anymore."

"Dang it," Thom said as he smacked himself in the head.

"I'll keep my eyes peeled for anything in the area. Really sorry. It just seemed the sellers wanted to seal the deal asap."

"Gotcha. So, I guess we're going to hold-off selling the Toronto home until I get back and find something else," Thom said.

"I'll leave a message if I see anything that requires immediate attention," Chris said.

"Okay, thanks Chris. Damn reception. Cell phones are such a waste of time and money," Thom complained. "I'll talk to you when I'm back in Ontario."

"Okay, Thom. So sorry about being the bearer of bad news," Chris said.

"No problem, talk to you soon. Bye, Chris," Thom said.

"Bye, Thom," Chris said, and they both hung up the phones.

Thom sat in the cafe in a state of bewilderment. He was upset at himself. He should have known not to wait on closing a deal or trying to seal a deal across the country in the first place. He should have turned his phone on. He should have at least checked the messages. He and the girls would need to remain in the Toronto home for the time being. Another few more months of memories in that old two-storey house. He thought that hopefully he would be able to find something quickly once they got back into Toronto and started looking. Thom took a deep breath and took a sip of coffee, then leaned back in his chair.

The staff kitchen and lounge at town hall were like any other staff room out there; a fridge, sink, microwave, and a few cupboards, but what made it unique were all the different posters of Banff lining the upper walls. Jeff, Rob, and Pete were eating lunch at one of the tables and were talking about sports when Barb came in.

"What's up, you jackasses?" Barb joked. "We got tickets to Titanic for tonight, everything else was sold out."

"Nice to see you too," Rob said sarcastically.

"I've seen it already," Pete said.

"We've all seen it," Jeff said.

"It was a pretty good flick," Rob said. "I'd see it again."

"I think everyone is on board to see it again. I just came to see if it's okay with you oafs," Barb said laughing.

"Whatever," Jeff said, shaking his head. "I could care less."

"Fine. As long as I can paint you naked," Pete said as he mimicked Rose lounging.

"You don't have a big enough canvas," Barb joked back.

Everyone laughed.

"I want you to paint me, Barb," Pete joked.

"I'm heading out early, so I'll see you stooges at the Saltlik around 6:00pm," Barb said as she walked away.

"Titanic again?" Pete whined.

"It was a pretty good flick," Rob said.

"Plenty of room on that door in the end," Jeff said. "Jack Dawson did not need to die."

"Well, on the plus side, we get to see Rose again," Rob said as he moved his eyebrows up and down.

Thom called his firm and got some details about a few upcoming projects that didn't inspire him at all. The only thing that truly excited him was seeing Titanic with Lacy that evening. He couldn't remember the last time he had been to the movies. Maybe it was five years earlier when he and the kids went to see Jurassic Park, but he couldn't be sure. Thom thought it was neat that this group of friends still made time to go to the movies together.

Thom had brought plenty of clothes with him, but he wanted to look his absolute best tonight and thought about going to pick out a new outfit. He closed his datebook, turned off his phone, gathered his things, and headed out the café doors. As he was walking, he remembered what his grief counsellor had told him about making big decisions. Although the mortgage had fallen through on the house in Caledon, he realized it wasn't such a bad thing; he would have more time to contemplate his future ambitions in the real estate market and weigh his options. His new goal today, however, was a fancy shirt that screamed classy, but not too classy.

Thom found a nice men's store that carried everything from casual to formal wear. He smiled and walked through the front doors. "Perfect!" he yelled as three different puzzled clerks turned to look at him.

"How can we help?" one of the clerks said with a smile.

"Something nice, not too scrubby and not too fancy-schmancy," Thom said.

"Got a hot date?" another clerk asked.

"In fact, I do," Thom proudly said. "I want to dress to impress."

"Nice," the male clerk said, shaking his head. "I got just the thing, brah. Follow me."

Thom smiled as he followed the clerk in anticipation.

Lacy walked everywhere in the summer months, including to and from work. She was almost home after a relatively easy day at the office and was feeling super positive about the night ahead. She loved hanging out with Barb, Tammy, Jeff, Pete, and Rob. Though she didn't know Thom well, she knew he was likeable, social, smart, dedicated, and obviously strong-willed following a difficult couple of emotional years.

Lacy had boyfriends in the past, but never had enough trust in them to make the next step. She was somewhat forced into independence at 18, when she left her parent's house for greener pastures. Lacy's early childhood was in rural Saskatchewan, and she desperately wanted to be a part of something greater than feeding chickens and sowing wheat. She left for Calgary in 1983 and never looked back. At Christmas time she would visit her parents, but often found it to be a chore, rather than a pleasure. Her parents were plain, sometimes boring, and obviously a product of war times. Negativity oozed from the board and batten.

Lacy's father had served for the Canadian Corps in World War II and did two excruciating, traumatic tours in Europe and had to endure the transition of returning to civilian life. He was quiet, reserved, and very rarely said two words, other than "When's supper?" or "Bedtime." The only story he ever told Lacy about the war was V-day when they all poured onto the streets in celebration of the allied victory in Europe.

Lacy's mom was also a product of growing up having to work hard all her life. She was born and raised in rural Saskatchewan where she raised animals her whole life and never, ever had a desire to leave. Lacy knew that both her parents would never change, and they would be happy living the exact same way the rest of their lives.

As Lacy walked carrying her briefcase and purse, she was thinking about cleaning her house, in case Barb, Tammy, or any other company came over after the movie. The friends would often gather at Lacy's place because it was the biggest and had a nice, scenic backyard overlooking the beautiful Mount Rundle. When she got home, Bob and his dog Hank were sitting on their front porch.

"Good afternoon, Lacy-bear. How was your day?" Bob asked as Lacy hurried up her steps.

"Another busy one. How about yours?" Lacy asked as she scratched Hank's head and behind his ears.

"Every day, I can't help but be thankful for everything I have. It truly is a magical world, Lacy-beans. I am thankful for my health, my family, and my wonderful friends and neighbours," Bob reflected.

"I feel the same way, Bob. Sometimes I get wrapped up in the complexities of the world and dwell on negative things, but every time I climb a mountain or look at this view it snaps me right out of the funk I'm in."

"Well said, young lady, well said," Bob said as he nodded his head and patted Hank on the head.

"See you soon, Bob," Lacy said as she headed inside her place. She closed the door and thought of all things she needed to do before meeting the gang at the pub before the movie. She flung off her shoes, threw down her bags and went up the stairs to get ready.

Back at the lodge, Thom was watching some T.V. and he was cleaning up and starting to get ready for the night. The door swung open, and Bella and Charlotte came through laughing and shoving each other. They each carried shopping bags and were flush red with sunshine and exercise. Thom smiled and thought about how much more positive their behaviour was since coming from the huge, gruelling, and often demanding world of Toronto. The girls had never come home in this state before.

"So, did you find what you were looking for?" asked Thom.

"Certainly did!" Bella exclaimed.

"We bought some cute outfits," Charlotte said.

"So did I," Thom said. "I grabbed a pizza while I was out, if you want a slice."

Bella and Charlotte both grabbed a slice and were clearly hungry because they both didn't say anything until they were both finished eating. Thom, meanwhile, slipped into the bathroom, changed, combed his hair, shaved, and brushed his teeth. When he came out, he took a deep breath. "Going to see Titanic tonight. I hope it's good. Wish me luck. Remember, don't be too late. Here's a few bucks." Thom went into his wallet and gave each of the girls a few small bills. "Be safe, no drugs, and no getting into the car with anyone who's been drinking."

"Yes, Dad," Charlotte said.

"Of course, Dad," Bella followed.

"Have fun. Remember punk rock is an attitude. Stick it to the man," Thom said as he thought he was being funny.

"Bye Dad," Charlotte said, rolling her eyes.

Thom made his way out the door as Bella and Charlotte began to get ready for the night.

The Saltlik was a casual fine-dining restaurant that had a very cozy, relaxing atmosphere. It served everything from gnocchi to prime Alberta beef. Its interior was lodge style, with large wooden trusses and a central fireplace. Booths outlined the dining area with a lounge/bar area near the front of the establishment.

Jeff, Rob, and Pete were at the Saltlik having a few martinis in the leather lounge chairs while they waited for Lacy, Barb, Tammy, and Thom to arrive. They chatted about the usual things; weather, the Calgary Stampeders, the economy, and the Clinton/Lewinski scandal. The three guys were more into the idea of having a few drinks, rather than seeing a three-hour movie they've already seen, but they were fine with it, it didn't bother them at all.

Barb, Tammy, and Lacy arrived together and joined the guys at their table. "Hi ladies," Pete said with a smile.

"Hi guys," Tammy replied. "Mind if we join you?"

"Not at all," Jeff said. "The three of you look terrific."

"You're not so bad yourselves," Barb said cheekily.

"Lacy, is Thom still coming?" Rob asked.

"Last time I saw him, he said he was," Lacy said.

Just as Lacy finished speaking, Thom came through the Saltlik doors, looking fresh, clean, and handsome. He had slicked his hair back, shaved his face and was dressed in some classy attire, including the new shirt he bought earlier in the day. He was feeling good, but still nervous, as he wanted to impress Lacy and make a good impression.

"Hey Thom," Rob said.

"Hi everyone," Thom said as he made eye contact with Lacy. She was looking so good. She had worn a casual but classy dress, done her hair and make-up and carried a certain confidence that made Thom crazy. It made him feel like a kid again, like when he first started to court Val. Similar as it was, it was completely different.

"How was the museum?" Lacy asked Thom.

"I thought it was great. The girls; not so much. They'd rather chat about Mariah Carey than learn about the receding glaciers of Canada's first national park," Thom said.

Everyone chuckled, which made Thom feel a little more relaxed. The new friends made their way to a large booth that sat everyone comfortably. They ordered a smorgasbord of food that they all shared, shrimp cocktails, nachos, hummus dip, chicken wings, and some sliders.

Thom had a chance to talk to Lacy, as she sat beside him. They talked about local tourism, upcoming Banff projects, Toronto, Lacy's upbringing in Saskatchewan, his home deal falling through, Thom's engineering firm, and, of course, Bella and Charlotte. It seemed that almost everything came back to his girls. Lacy adored this about Thom, his love, his adoration, and his commitment to his daughter's wellbeing. Lacy found herself trusting Thom more and more with each passing minute. Lacy, a very attractive, successful woman very seldom found herself in a position where she felt a man to be trustworthy, so it was something that was a long time coming. She knew what most men's intentions were and did not feel that type of vibe from Thom. He listened, he cared, he had a sense of humour, and he was independent; all qualities which were a rare combination in men. There was a rare feeling inside Lacy that allowed her to somehow feel at ease and lean back.

Everyone had a couple drinks and were feeling warm and fuzzy as the sun went down behind the distant mountains. It was Pete's turn to grab the bill, which he was more than willing to pay. The entire gang waited out front of the establishment for Pete to finish paying. Once he came outside, the seven friends made their way down the street to the movie theatre. It was a beautiful, colourful Monet sky as they strolled down Bear Street together.

Brody sat in the lobby of the lodge waiting for Charlotte and Bella to come down. He was content to just wait; he didn't need to fidget with anything or tap his fingers or toes, he just liked thinking about the night ahead. He, like everyone else this evening, decided to dress up for the night ahead. He wore a long sleeve black shirt with a single 3-inch white stripe running across his chest, something right off the cover of Tiger Beat magazine. He even wore his best khaki pants, which were only reserved for special occasions.

Charlotte and Bella came downstairs, and Brody's eyes locked on Bella. She looked dreamy. Her hair was done, her summer outfit sparkled, and her lips were captivating. It made Brody even crazier for Bella.

"You two look great," Brody said with a cotton mouth as his eyes fixed on Bella.

"Thanks," Charlotte said.

"I love your dress, Bella," Brody complimented.

"This old thing," Bella joked. "Sorry we're late." She wasn't sorry at all. She wanted Brody to watch her coming down the stairs. Bella was feeling just as nervous as Brody was.

"So, how was your day?" Brody asked the girls.

Charlotte and Bella looked at each other and laughed as they both thought about trying on all those ridiculous cowboy outfits. "It was lovely. We did a little shopping, got some lunch, saw the sights, all in all, very relaxing," Bella said.

"That sounds nice," Brody said.

"So, are you two ready to go?" Charlotte asked as she couldn't help but think of Zach as she noticed the connection between Bella and Brody.

"Yeah, let's get out of here," Brody said.

The three walked a couple of blocks to the Rose and Crown. Banff was such a small little town; you could walk practically anywhere in 15 minutes. The Rose and Crown was no exception.

Zach was waiting outside the bar by himself. He was leaning against the brick wall, wearing cargo shorts and a Pearl Jam t-shirt. He clearly didn't put in as much effort as Charlotte did, but she didn't care that he didn't care. It made him all the more attractive and punk rock.

"So glad you made it!" Zach shouted as Charlotte, Bella and Brody strolled down the sidewalk. "Shows about to start! Follow me!" he said as he flipped his blonde hair over his shoulder.

Zach led Charlotte, Bella, and Brody up the stairs to the large pub on the second floor. Zach told the bouncer working that these were his friends and he let them pass right through. The stage was set up in the corner of the large, packed room. It was a young crowd, however there were adults sprinkled throughout the place. Most of the young people were standing in and around the one-foot elevated stage. Zach and his friends had a long banquet table they were sitting at and saved a few seats for Charlotte, Bella, and Brody.

"Have a seat, grab some drinks. I'll be right back," Zach said as he made his way through the crowd and up onto the stage.

"Where is he going?" Charlotte said laughing.

"Is he in the band?" Brody asked.

"I don't think so," Charlotte replied.

All three were puzzled about Zach's spontaneous move toward the stage. Once he was on stage, he picked up the microphone. "Ladies and Gentlemen, boys and girls, children of all ages, welcome to the Rose and Crown." The crowd cheered. "The best pub in the best town in Canada!" The crowd cheered again. "Tonight's performers stem all the way from Stoner, British Columbia. Would you please put your hands together for Stoner Haze!" The crowd went bananas for the small-town band. Three members came out from the hallway behind the bar, picked up their instruments and began playing the 'Blitzkrieg Bop' by the Ramones.

Zach moved back off stage and went to the bar and got a picture of beer and four plastic cups. He was head banging to the rhythm of the music as he made his way back to the table where Charlotte, Bella, and Brody were.

The girls weren't expecting to have any alcohol tonight, but certainly welcomed it considering they were underage and had no adult supervision.

"So, what do you think?!" Zach yelled loud enough so everyone at the table could hear.

"Stoner Haze. Funny name," Charlotte said, smiling at Zach.

"Righteous, eh?" Zach said as he poured the cheap lager into the four plastic glasses.

"This place is great," Bella yelled into Brody's ear.

"Live music every night," Brody yelled back.

"Cheers everyone!" Zach raised his glass.

"Cheers!" Everyone said together as they raised their glasses.

The Lux cinema was a modest building that blended into the rest of Banff architecture. It had four theatres and showed, not only the newest from Hollywood, but foreign and Canadian films, special interest productions, and documentaries.

In theatre four, Titanic was in full swing, and Jeff, Barb, Tammy, Lacy, Thom, Pete, and Rob sat watching the chaos about to unfold as the night watchman from the Titanic yelled 'Iceberg, right ahead.'

"Ok, buckle up Tommy boy, things are about to get rough for the people aboard the unsinkable Titanic," Pete said, leaning into Thom.

"Would you shut up down there?" Tammy loudly whispered.

"Shhh," Rob retorted.

Thom was enjoying himself immensely. It had been so long since he had been to the movies. Every now and then, Lacy would look to see what Thom's reaction would be to certain moments.

"God, this is going to suck," Thom said to Lacy.

Lacy laughed. "You do know how this ends, don't you?"

"Shhh, don't spoil it," Thom joked.

The iceberg crashed into the side of the Titanic and Thom's mouth dropped. Lacy turned to look at him and she laughed at his jaw-dropping reaction.

Stoner Haze finished their opening set with a cover of 'London Calling' by The Clash. The warm, stale beer was starting to have its effects on Charlotte and Zach. Bella and Brody were clearly not as interested in drinking as Charlotte was. She chugged the final half of her beer and let out a little burp.

"Excuse me!" Charlotte laughed. "It's good stuff."

"Hey, you want to go get some fresh air?" Zach asked Charlotte.

"Yeah, sure," she responded as Zach grabbed her hand and they headed downstairs.

"So, do you like the band?" Bella asked Brody.

"They are pretty sweet. Are you having a good time?" Brody responded.

"Yeah! It's nice to hang out with some people my own age," Bella said with a smile.

"I hear you. I'm the youngest worker at the lodge, everyone is way older than me," Brody said.

Charlotte and Zach barged through the front doors with energy and excitement. The front sidewalk was crammed with young people smoking cigarettes.

"You having a good time, good Charlotte?" Zach said as he mimicked bowing like a royal.

"Why, yes, my good man," she said as she grabbed his hands and raised him up. They locked eyes as they both pulled each other closer and moved in for a kiss. The young couple did not stand out a bit, as a few other couples were not afraid of showing their affection in public either.

Charlotte felt her blood boiling as the alcohol mixed with combined with the heightened emotions almost paralyzed her. Once they pulled out of the kiss, they opened their eyes to the sight of each other smiling.

"That was nice," Charlotte said.

"Want to do it again?" Zach asked cordially.

"Yes," she said as they embraced again.

Bella and Brody had made their way to the pool table and were engaged in a friendly game of 8-ball. Clearly Bella hadn't played, whereas Brody loved pool. He and his dad and him had been coming here for chicken wings and pizza since he was a little boy.

"Do you want me to start playing with my left hand?" Brody joked.

"Just you wait; I'm making a comeback," Bella said, aimed, shot, and completely missed the ball.

"Nice try," Brody laughed.

"No need to mock me," Bella snapped.

"Try holding your hand like this," Brody said as he demonstrated a proper bridge technique on the pool table and Bella nestled close to him and tried to do the same.

Charlotte and Zach came back into the Rose and Crown and met Bella and Brody at the pool table carrying another pitcher of beer. Bella looked at them holding hands and almost immediately knew what had happened outside. Bella gave them both a smile in acknowledgement and went back to her pool shot.

Thom watched as the old lady Rose threw the priceless gem back into the ocean at the end of the Titanic. By this point of the movie Thom was in tears. Lacy and the rest of the gang had already gone through the emotions of the blockbuster and were not fazed by the dramatic intensity. Thom, however, knew about losing someone you loved; having to let go was the hardest thing that he has ever had to endure. It truly was a metaphor for his life, he thought. He needed to live the best life he possibly could. He needed to respect everything Val ever did for him, move on, but never let go of her memory.

Lacy looked at Thom crying and couldn't help but become emotional herself. She could see the thousand thoughts running through his head. She reached out and grabbed his hand on the armrest. He turned to Lacy and smiled. "What a beautiful ending," he said as he turned back to the screen to avoid the embarrassment of Lacy seeing him cry.

Lacy knew Thom was a widower and this reminder of love and love-lost must have been particularly emotional for him. She wanted to hug him. He thought of Val's final days as she slowly passed away; her cold hands, the tests, her weakening state, and the melancholy of having to let go. "I can't believe she threw the necklace into the sea," Thom said as laughter blended with his tears.

"There was plenty of room on that wood door," Rob yelled down to Thom.

"If Jack got on that door, he would have killed them both," Barb yelled back.

"They could have at least tried," Tammy said.

"What an epic movie," Thom said to Lacy.

"Want to get out of here?" she said with a smile.

Rob, Pete, Jeff, Tammy, Barb, Lacy, and Thom all got up and made their way outside with the rest of the theatregoers. As they were walking out, Thom couldn't help but feel euphoria as he thought about how Val would want him to move on and live the best possible life. She would want him to meet new people and try new things, as he would want the same for her if he was the one who had.

The friends all said good night and parted ways, except for Thom and Lacy who continued to chat and reflect on the movie.

"It's a beautiful night. Can I walk you home?" Thom asked.

"We don't get much crime here. It's pretty safe," Lacy said.

"What about the late-night grizzly bears?" Thom joked.

"You're pretty good at fending off bears, are you?" she said.

"Been doing it for years," Thom said as he flexed his muscles.

Lacy laughed as the two strolled down the quiet street.

The B.C. band Stoner Haze rocked the night away as the room got hazier and sweatier with each passing minute. Brody had his arms wrapped around Bella as the two watched the final few songs of the band. Charlotte and Zach were clearly intoxicated, as they sat at the back table and made out with no regard for anyone around them. Charlotte had tried tequila for the first time and was on the verge of blacking out.

The band finished with 'God Save The Queen' by The Sex Pistols which caused the crowd to erupt in applause. Zach, in a drunken, but still energized state, ran up on stage. "Give it up for Stoner Haze! Don't forget to tip your servers and bartenders! Goodnight, everybody!"

Zach jumped off stage as the lights came up in the pub. He made his way back to the table where Charlotte, Bella, and Brody waited.

"That was so hot," Charlotte slurred.

"Okay, best we get back to the lodge," Bella said in a motherly tone.

"Here's my number, Charlotte. Call me tomorrow," Zach said with one eye partially closed.

"Goodnight, Zach. I will miss you," Charlotte said slowly.

"Okay. Goodnight Zach. Great job. We'll see you around," Bella said as she grabbed Charlotte and led her down the stairs. "Grab onto the handrail, you nerd."

"I'm not a nerd," Charlotte said in a drunken defensive manner.

"You're right. You're a boozy lush," she said as Charlotte stumbled out the front door.

They took a few steps down the sidewalk before Charlotte stopped suddenly. "I'm gonna puke. Oh god, it's coming. My mouth is watering."

She turned toward the nearest flower bed and puked almost entirely liquid, while Brody and Bella did their best to cover her and her dignity.

Lacy and Thom were holding hands as they approached Lacy's place. "Well, this is my humble little abode," Lacy said as she presented her quaint little mountain home.

Thom grabbed Lacy by the hands. "I've had the best week of my life, thanks to you. The girls are behaving like girls again. They've been open and honest; they've been social, and they've been great company," Thom said honestly. "It keeps getting better and better. I want to thank you for everything you've done for me and the girls. I know we've only just met, but it seems like I've known you my whole life."

"So, do you want to come in for a drink, or what?" Lacy asked.

"That sounds great," Thom said as they strolled into Lacy's place.

Charlotte's arm was around Bella's shoulder as she flung her onto the lodge bed. "You disgust me," Bella said. "This is the only time I'm ever going to do this."

"Can you get me some water?" Charlotte said in a baby voice.

"This is why Dad loves me more than you."

"My mouth tastes like crap," Charlotte said, smacking her lips.

Bella brought Charlotte a glass of water. "You've got puke all over you." She helped Charlotte drink the water and get into pyjamas.

"I kissed him. We kissed a lot," Charlotte said, still slurring her words.

"Go to sleep. You're going to feel like hot death in the morning. I'll leave water on your nightstand," Bella said with a smile.

Charlotte fell asleep almost instantly. Bella walked about the room, brushed her teeth, combed her hair, and got into bed thinking mostly about Brody, but also where her dad might be. Before long, Bella and Charlotte were sound asleep.

Chapter 9 - Aftermath

Bella woke around 8:00am. She did her typical stretch and yawn and opened the blinds letting the early morning light into the room, making Charlotte stir. Charlotte gave a ridiculous dinosaur yawn and moan making Bella laugh.

"Welcome to your first beeriod," Bella joked.

Charlotte moaned, rolled over and put a pillow over her head. "I hate you."

"What's the matter, whittle sister?" Bella said in a baby voice.

"My mouth tastes like ass," Charlotte said removing the pillow from her face.

"Halitosis can break up relationships," Bella laughed as she made her bed.

"Can you get me a glass of water? Petty pwease," Charlotte asked, giving the pouty lip.

"You are useless."

"Where is dad?" asked Charlotte.

"He left this note. It says: *Bella and Char, come to the summit of Tunnel Mountain. Just down the road. Should take you an hour. Pack a couple of snacks and bring plenty of water. I'll be at the top waiting for you. - Dad*"

"You're telling me I have to move?" Charlotte moaned.

"Get up sissy," Bella said. "Let's get moving. Get in the shower and brush that awful mouth."

"What happened last night? I don't remember much. Just being at the bar and drinking that awful beer. The band I remember kind of too," Charlotte said, putting the pieces together.

"You puked in the flowerbed outside St. Paul's Presbyterian Church," Bella said, laughing. "You stumbled home, and you kept saying: 'I love him. I love Zach'. You were so hammered. I've never seen you like that."

"I don't plan on being like that again," Charlotte said in her most convincing voice.

"We'll see about that," Bella said, rolling her eyes. "Let's get moving."

The girls proceeded to get cleaned up and head up the road to Tunnel Mountain; a small, beginner hike compared to some of the gargantuan mountains surrounding Banff. Tunnel Mountain had a long and winding road that led to the town campground; it was busy at this time of year and the girls admired all the sights, sounds, and smells of the morning campers preparing their breakfasts.

With each step Charlotte took, she began to feel better, but it was a painful process. It was a cloudy day, truly reflecting how Charlotte felt.

"How about some pickled pork lips?" asked Bella. "What about some egg salad sandwiches?"

"Would you shut your disgusting mouth!" snapped Charlotte.

"How about liver and onions, or sheep stomach stuffed with oatmeal and kidneys?" Bella was having too much fun. Each time she mentioned something gross, Charlotte would do a little dry heave.

"I'm gonna punch you in the tit," Charlotte threatened, and Bella just laughed.

Thom waited at the top of the mountain with Lacy. They hadn't left each other's side since the night before. Thom had stayed the night at Lacy's place. They had already been out for breakfast and were planning to part ways soon, as Lacy was headed to work.

The view from the summit was a beautiful one, looking west down at the village of Banff. Both Thom and Lacy stared off into the distance as the morning sun hit their faces.

"I've had a great night and morning. Can I call you later?" Thom asked.

"I've had a blast too. I'm glad you liked Titanic." Lacy gave a little giggle. "Call me tonight. Maybe we can make plans for the weekend."

"That sounds great."

"Maybe we could go to Lake Louise in a few days," Lacy suggested.

"That sounds like a plan."

"I gotta get going. Tell the girls I said 'hey'," Lacy said, as she stood up and tightened her backpack. Thom rose to his feet and the two embraced and kissed each other.

"Bye," Thom said.

"Bye," Lacy said as she turned and started back down the trail.

Thom couldn't help but think of all that had happened in the past week. Both him and his daughters had taken incredible steps in the recovery process. He hadn't thought about another woman until he saw Lacy in the coffee shop. Was it possible to fall in love twice in Banff? Were his girls falling in love too? Why was Banff such a force in his life? He couldn't remember a better week.

Thom watched Lacy walk down until she was out of sight. He then smiled from ear to ear. He sat back down on a nearby rock and took a long drink from his water bottle. Thom pulled out his cell phone from his backpack and turned it on. He was doing his best to try and remain responsible. He noticed there were no messages, so he turned it off and shoved it back into his knapsack.

Bella and Charlotte came over the last outcropping of Tunnel Mountain and saw their dad sitting in deep contemplation.

"Dad!" Bella shouted.

"Girls!" Thom shouted.

"Hey," Charlotte moaned.

"We just saw Lacy. Did you come up here together?" Bella asked.

"Yeah, we've already been to breakfast too," Thom replied. "So, welcome to the top of Tunnel Mountain. What do you think?"

"It's great, dad," Bella said.

"So cool," Charlotte added.

Thom smiled as his girls looked out onto the village of Banff. He knew they had had a late night and probably were feeling the aftermath, so he didn't want to agitate them. "So, me and Lacy were talking and thought maybe the four of us could go to Lake Louise in a couple of days and have a nice dinner later that evening," Thom suggested.

"Sounds good to me," Char said.

"Me too. Let's do it," Bella said.

A month ago, neither one of the girls would have agreed so suddenly or so enthusiastically. They were both excited for their father and were beginning to see him as a vulnerable, authentic, human being, rather than a parental authority figure that fed, housed, and disciplined them throughout their childhood. In their early years, their father was a superhero; a man who could never get hurt, he would carry them on his shoulders, use magic or humour to cheer them up, or surprise them at the most unexpected times. They were starting to see his humanity, his faults, his insecurities, his passions, and his capacity for caring and understanding.

"I'm glad you are meeting new people, Dad," Charlotte said seriously.

"Thanks honey. Lacy and I have a lot in common," Thom said, as he was taken aback by his daughter's comments.

"Just remember we're going back to Toronto," Bella said, as she thought about Brody and the melancholy that she would have to endure when she left to go back to Ontario.

"I know Lacy and I are going to keep in touch. We've been open and honest about ourselves and feelings. We're going to talk on the phone and send each other electronic mail," Thom replied.

"Bella's going to have to say goodbye to Brody too," Charlotte said.

"Would you shut your cornhole?" Bella snapped back.

"It's good to be open and honest with him," Thom advised. "Talking on the phone isn't such a bad thing."

"I know, I know. He wants to come visit Toronto when the Stampeders play the Argonauts in November," Bella said.

"Well, that would be fun," Thom said. "He could always stay at our place...on the couch of course."

Charlotte took a big drink of water. Though they hadn't hiked very far, she was sweating more than usual. She was looking quite pale as she put her hands on her knees. "Can we rest awhile?" she said, "My brain hurts."

"Everything okay, Char?" Thom asked.

"Yeah, just a little winded," Charlotte said, trying to change the subject quickly. "I think I'm just really hungry."

Bella gave Charlotte a little nudge which threw her off balance. Charlotte was clearly annoyed by her sister taking advantage of her condition. Charlotte kept telling herself last night was the last time she was ever going to drink tequila. Just the sight of the bottle might make her heave. Bella thought it was hilarious that Charlotte was so vulnerable. Very rarely would Bella get to take advantage of such situations. Charlotte was usually alert, physically capable, and able to defend herself in most situations; today was a little different.

"So how was the concert last night? Did you girls have fun?"

"Charlotte certainly had a fun, eventful night," Bella snickered. "Brody and I had a blast too. He taught me how to play pool."

"Fun!" Thom said.

"It was good. The band played a bunch of punk covers; Fugazi, Sex Pistols, The Clash, you know, all the hits," Charlotte said.

"She and Zach really hit it off," Bella announced.

"He's a cool boy. He was the M.C. of the show," Charlotte said.

Charlotte was doing her best to keep it together. Thom had already figured out they had done some drinking last night, but he wasn't upset. He was young once. Thom knew it was best to ignore the fact and play dumb.

"Sounds like everyone had a blast. What do you say we go grab a bite to eat and have a nice, relaxing, lazy afternoon?" Thom suggested.

"Perfect idea," Charlotte responded.

"Okay great, let's get out of here," Thom said as they all made their way back down the mountain.

Chapter 10 - Lake Louise

T he morning began with a hearty breakfast at the lodge; eggs, bacon, hash browns, toast, and fresh fruit. Jim, Brody's father, even hand delivered the food to Thom and the girls as they eagerly awaited their breakfast. Both Charlotte and Bella were extremely excited about the road trip through the Rocky Mountains to Lake Louise; famous for its beautiful, turquoise-coloured water.

Charlotte was feeling much better and certainly wiser on this morning. The three hot showers she had over the past 24 hours helped to purge any remnants of the darkness that was tequila. Charlotte had called Zach and they laughed about their zany escapades at the Rose and Crown. He mentioned he puked later on that evening and blamed the tequila for all his misgivings, which made Charlotte feel much better.

Bella also had a phone conversation with Brody the night before. They laughed a lot about Charlotte and the walk home, as well as her march up Tunnel Mountain. Today, Brody was driving into Red Deer to pick up a massive order of Prime Alberta beef his mother and father special ordered. It was a long trip, and he wouldn't return until later that night.

After breakfast, Thom and the girls left to pick up Lacy at her house. The forecast called for clear skies and calm conditions, which was perfect for a hike in and around Lake Louise. It was about an hour drive, so Thom stopped and picked up a couple of coffees for he and Lacy and some teas for the girls. When they got to her house, Thom got out and was about to knock on the door, when Lacy swung the door open.

"Good morning, sunshine!" Lacy said with a smile.

"You look terrific." Thom was a little startled. Even if she had been wearing a paper bag and 10-gallon cowboy hat, he would have complimented her, but he ultimately admired her west-coast style and perfectly unkept hair. He wanted to kiss her, but knew it wasn't a good time, as both his daughters were staring at them.

"Thanks, you guys all set?" Lacy asked. "Plenty of water? Towels? Change of socks?"

"You know it," Thom replied, "I brought you a cappuccino from The Bean, just how you like it."

"You're the best. Just let me get my bag and we can hit the road," she said as she stepped back inside.

Thom felt like he was floating. The stars were finally aligning. The girls were both in good moods, sunshine was pouring down, and he was about to go hiking with the girl of his dreams. Thom made his way to the car and stuck his head through the window and looked at both the girls. "Please, be on your best behaviour. She's an important lady and I like her very much. Do not screw this up for me. Thank you very much."

Bella hated him for saying that, but somewhat understood his rationale and sarcasm. Charlotte didn't think too deeply about it. If anything, it reminded Charlotte not to speak what was directly on her mind. She still remembered what her grade 8 teacher said: "Stop, think, then speak." It was a great rule that seemed to have stuck with Charlotte. From that time forward, when boys and girls spoke out impulsively, Charlotte would feel genuine embarrassment for them not knowing how to restrain themselves or think before speaking. Charlotte loved silence and thinking to herself.

"Thanks, Dad," Bella said as she rolled her eyes.

"No problem, Pops," said Charlotte as she rolled down the window. "Lacy's the bomb. She's one cool cat."

Lacy came outside, shut her front door, jumped from her top step, and landed with an energetic smile.

"Clearly, she's excited," Bella slyly observed.

Lacy dropped her bag in the trunk then sat in the front seat. Thom handed her the steamy Americano with cream. "Perfect," she said, "Mmm. Thank you." Lacy turned to the girls in the backseat. "Good morning. How are things going, ladies?"

"Pretty good," Bella said in a neutral tone.

"I'm excited to get this show on the road," Charlotte said in her best vaudeville voice.

"Me too. I have a great day mapped out. You three are going to love this route around Lake Louise," Lacy said as she turned around and smiled at Thom. "I've only done it once, but it was an absolute blast."

"Amazing," Thom said as he put the car in drive, and they made their way to the main highway. Instead of heading east toward Calgary, they were heading northwest into the interior. The further they got, the bigger and more unique the mountains became.

Charlotte and Bella felt like they were little kids again. They just sat silent and marvelled at the wonders outside their windows. They passed Castle Mountain that resembled something out of mediaeval lore. The peaks, still covered in snow, resembled multiple turrets atop a towering castle. What shocked both girls the most, were the seemingly infinite miles of pristine forest and mountains. The crowded, congested streets of Toronto seemed so far off. These wide-open natural spaces ignited their imaginations and took years of stress off their adolescent shoulders.

Thom and Lacy were just as happy in the silence as the girls were. Every now and then, Thom would glance in the rearview mirror to watch the girls marvelling at the mountains, rivers, and forests.

Lacy pulled a CD out of her jacket pocket that was clearly marked with handwritten songs; everything from Built to Spill to Modest Mouse, Massive Attack to The Weakerthans. Though she was old in the eyes of Bella and Charlotte, she was 'cool'.

"I just burned this road trip mix. Mind if I pop it in?" Lacy asked.

"Go for it," Thom enthusiastically agreed.

Lacy pulled the CD out and popped it in the car stereo and then handed back the case to the girls. "I don't know if you'll like it or not, but there's some great bands on here."

Bella reached out and grabbed the case. She recognized Modest Mouse, as Brody couldn't stop talking about them. "I've heard of a few of these bands."

Charlotte snatched the case from Bella. She took a quick look too. "I haven't heard of any of these bands. No Limp Biscuit?"

"Absolutely not," Lacy said in a serious tone and Thom laughed.

The first song came on and instantly provided a euphoric, road trip atmosphere. Both Charlotte and Bella felt giddy with optimism as they heard songs they had never heard before. Song after song, they felt perfectly comfortable staring off into the vastness of space. Listening to the new music reminded them of humanity's energy and connection to one another.

The rest of the car ride to Lake Louise was the soundtrack of their lives. Each song hit everyone in a unique way. When either Bella or Charlotte heard a song they really liked, they would double, sometimes triple check the song and band they were listening to. To Bella and Charlotte, life had basically been filled with Top 40 hits: Janet Jackson, Whitney Houston, Elton John, Madonna, and Celine Dion. Combined with their recent concert, this indie CD was a gateway into music from around the world, not just the dolled-up, dominant pop of the day, but artists playing their own instruments, singing their own songs, slugging it out on the streets. Grunge had played a role in their early adolescence, but they were now heading into adulthood and this alternative music was speaking to them.

Thom was elated that his girls were pulling out of the almost year-long depression they had found themselves in. Watching them look out the car window listening to music, Thom could sense the beginning of their acceptance of their mother's passing. Knowing they were meeting new people, trying new things, and not falling into despair or depression was such a relief for Thom.

Eventually, their car pulled off the Trans-Canada Highway into Lake Louise. The long and winding road had a few large lodges that built of stone and timber and, seemingly, were very busy at this time of the year. There wasn't much to the area except for the large Fairmont Lake Louise Hotel, which was built around the time of the Fairmont Banff Springs Hotel. The large hotel was surrounded by mountains and evergreen forest, as well as a few out-buildings sprinkled around it. Charlotte and Bella were in awe.

Though it had only been about a 50-minute drive, everyone was looking forward to getting out and stretching their legs. The parking lot only had a few cars which was a good sign. Thom parked the car, and everyone exited and got in some great stretches before they geared up and started their hike.

"I've got a really neat surprise," Lacy said as she was stretching toward the sky.

"If it's as good as that CD, I'm excited," Bella said.

"Dad, do you know what it is?" Charlotte asked.

"No clue," he said. "I'm certainly intrigued though."

"Everyone is going to have to wait a little bit. Don't worry, you'll love it," Lacy said to everyone.

The four of them walked through the parking lot and after only 100 metres, were confronted by the emerald-coloured Lake Louise. Rock flour had made its way along the Bow River and settled here at this lake, giving an almost fluorescent turquoise colour. It truly was striking; both Charlotte and Bella were amazed that such a place even existed.

After soaking in the initial shock and awe, the plan was a 12-mile hike, a loop around the shoreline of Lake Louise, then make their way back to the parking lot where they had started. The hike began off with a gradual incline through the pine groves of Lake Louise. After making their way up the valley and along various cliffs and outcroppings, passing waterfalls and streams, they made it to beautiful Lake Annette, which was much smaller than Lake Louise, but had a similar turquoise colour. Lake Annette also happened to have a small, pebbled beach. Everyone had worked up an incredible sweat from hiking in the sun and welcomed the idea of jumping into a cool body of water.

"Wanna go for a dip?" Lacy asked.

"How cold is it?" Bella asked.

"It is runoff from a glacier, so it's pretty cold," Lacy answered.

"I'm going in," Thom said as he flung off his shoes, socks, backpack, and shirt.

"Last one in is a rotten egg," Charlotte joked as she kicked off her shoes.

"Fine, I'm a rotten egg," Bella said as she folded her arms.

Charlotte and her dad ran into the water not expecting what was about to hit them. The two let out the same high-pitched squeal. Which made Lacy and Bella laugh.

"Don't worry, Bella, it is not a race with me. Let's go in at our own pace," Lacy said, as Bella smiled back. "I think those two are crazy. Just try putting your feet in. You won't regret it."

"That, I think I could handle," Bella said smiling.

Bella couldn't help but compare Lacy, in this moment, to her mother. Of course, she knew they were different people, but they shared common motherly instincts that Bella, of course, missed. They both had delicate sensibilities and approaches to situations, which for Bella was welcome.

Both Lacy and Bella took off their shoes and socks, dropped their backpacks and undressed down to their sports bras. By this point Thom and Charlotte were neck deep in the lake and still getting acclimated to the frigid waters. They were both taking long, concentrated deep breaths to help with the adjusting.

Bella dipped her toes in and immediately felt the coolness on her feet. After six tough miles through the rugged terrain, this almost felt like heaven. She hadn't realized how badly she was torturing her feet. The cool water helped relieve any pain she was feeling. Lacy was out further, with water up to her thighs.

"Come on out." Lacy said as she beckoned Bella.

"I think I'm good here," Bella insisted.

"Come, let's do it together," Lacy said.

"Fine," Bella crept deeper and deeper as she was hopping like a bunny. Finely she made it next to Lacy.

"Ready?" Lacy asked.

"Ready for what?" Bella responded.

"To dive in. Trust me. It makes it so much easier. Ready. One, two, three, go!" Both ladies took the brave plunge and came up screaming.

"Isn't that better?" Thom shouted.

"So cold. So cold," Bella said as she struggled to regain her breath.

"You get used to it, Bella," Charlotte said, trying to reassure her sister. "Breathe deep."

Everyone did get used to the glacial waters and they soon were refreshed and invigorated as the morning became afternoon. It was like getting a second wind. They all felt energized as they tread water for a few minutes, chatted, and shared some laughs. Eventually they made their way out of the water together feeling like a million bucks.

"Lake Annette, she's the coldest bitch I've come across," Bella joked as everyone laughed.

They all got dried off and prepared to hit the trail which looped back around to the Lake Louise shoreline. As they left, Bella turned back around wanting to solidify the memory of Lake Annette, Lacy's guidance, and the new light she was starting to see in her life.

After the six-mile, gradual descent down through Paradise Valley, they made it back to Lake Louise, which was just as stunning as when they first saw it. Bella and Charlotte made their way well ahead of Lacy and Thom who proceeded to chat about the girls and their growth over the past couple of months. They also talked about each other's work and other places they had visited in and around the Rocky Mountains.

Both Charlotte and Bella were restored by the cold plunge into Lake Annette and were clearly feeling positive.

"I really think Dad and Lacy are hitting it off," Charlotte said.

"I like her," Bella said.

"Me too. She's cool."

"The best part is that Dad really likes her."

"Do long distance relationships work?" Charlotte inquired.

"I'm really not sure," Bella said thinking about Brody.

The four hikers were now halfway around the lake and there was a fork in the trail ahead. Everyone was exhausted, as they had now travelled about 14 miles on rough terrain.

"Take a right!" Lacy yelled from behind.

The hikers made their way through the dense bush until they reached a small log cabin where an elderly couple was sitting at a table on the front porch. The girls were the first to see the oddity in the mountains and were lured by the homeyness and aromas permeating from the cabin.

Charlotte and Bella were taken aback that this was a quaint little restaurant in the middle of the mountains.

"Look! It's a restaurant!" Charlotte said as she saw the menu on a nearby post.

"It certainly is," the old man said to the girls.

"Amazing!" Bella responded.

"It's actually a teahouse," said the old lady.

This was Lacy's surprise for Thom and the girls. She had hoped it was just as shocking to Thom, Bella, and Charlotte as it was to her, the first time she stumbled upon The Plain of Six Glaciers Teahouse.

"What do you think?" Lacy asked the girls. "It surprised the heck out of me, the first time I was here."

"I thought it was a figment of my imagination," Charlotte said. "The Plain of Six Glaciers Teahouse," she said, reading the menu.

"It is like a desert mirage," Bella said. "Can we please stop here?"

"Duh, of course," Thom said sarcastically. "I could certainly go for a Six Glacier tea."

"They have the best teas, not just the orange pekoe junk. They also have the best snacks. Let's grab a table," Lacy said. "I'll go inside and let them know we're here."

The old couple was interested in all the energy the four hikers brought with them. The pair had been coming to this spot for decades and rarely saw young families. They were dressed in modern hiking gear, with matching headbands, making them the cutest couple.

Thom and Lacy admired them and their ability to have hiked all the way out to this remote location. They assumed the couple were around 75 years old but were truly amazed at how fit and joyful they appeared. Thom looked at Lacy as he unhitched his gear and sat at the table and couldn't help but compare himself to the elders who were obviously still in love after all these years. Lacy dropped her bag beside the table and looked at Thom, who was looking at her.

"What?" Lacy said smiling, as she walked in toward the cozy cabin.

"Nothing," Thom said as he looked down toward the menu on the table and smiled to himself.

"I want to try the raspberry leaf tea," Bella said.

"I'm looking at the apple cinnamon tea," Charlotte followed.

"So, how often do you come here?" Thom asked the couple.

"Try to get here every week," the old man said.

"I love the treats. I think it's homemade cranberry, walnut, and pecan muffins today," the old lady said, as the old man looked back at her with a timeless smile on his face.

"They have sandwiches too; peanut butter, cheese, cold cuts. Perfect little pit stop here among the mountains," the old man added.

Lacy came back to the table with four water bottles. It was nice for everyone to have a chair to sit in as it had been a long hike. They all leaned back and watched nature in all its sublime glory. Red-tailed squirrels were hard at work in every direction. Jays circled the cabin dashing in and out of the bird feeders the cabin owners had hung on nearby tree branches. Elk could also be heard off in the distance, as rutting season was just a few weeks away.

A middle-aged woman came out of the cabin and approached Thom's table. "Hello, my name is Susanne. This is my place. My mother Joy bought this place in 1959 and it has been in the family ever since. So happy you've joined us today."

"No kidding, eh? So, how do you get supplies and power out here?" Thom asked.

"No electricity and we carry in everything on our backs," Susanne said.

"Wow," Charlotte said. "That's commitment."

"They used to drive everything on pack horses, but we just minimalized and made it more of a snack house, than a restaurant."

"This would be a fun place to work," Bella said to Charlotte.

"Staff usually have a great time. We have chicken noodle soup and tuna fish sandwiches today. We also have fresh cranberry, walnut, and pecan muffins. Also, anything you see on the menu. Another thing, we only take cash. No electricity, so no credit cards," Susanne said with a shrug.

"Get anything you want. I've got enough cash," Thom said.

"I'll have the soup and one of the delish sounding muffins and an apple cinnamon tea," Charlotte said.

"Great," Susanne said as she wrote down the order.

"Can I please have a cheese sandwich and a raspberry leaf tea?" Bella asked.

"Ok," Susanne affirmed.

"I'll have a tuna fish sandwich and the soup, please, with a hot chocolate," Lacy said with a smile.

"Excellent," Susanne said nodding. "And for yourself?"

"I'll have the same as her," Thom said, indicating Lacy's order.

"Wonderful. I'll be back shortly with some drinks," Susanne said, as she went back to the cabin.

"I'm so excited about this," Charlotte said. "I want to live here."

"Me too," Thom said, in agreement.

The four hikers found themselves talking about working and living in Banff and surrounding areas, like Lake Louise. Lacy brought a deck of cards and taught the girls euchre as they sipped on their tea and hot chocolates in the fresh mountain air. Frustrated at first, Charlotte and Bella finally got used to the right and left bowers, making trump, following suit, and never trumping your partner's ace. When the food came, they put the cards to the side and munched their snacks with delight.

After the relaxing meal, Susanne cleared their table of the dirty dishes. "Can I get you anything else?" she asked.

"This has been so great, Susanne. Thanks for everything. Truly a diamond in the rough," Lacy said.

"No problem at all. I'm so happy to be here and meeting so many lovely folks. It's truly heaven on earth," Susanne said.

"You said it," Lacy said in agreement.

"I'll bring the bill by the table shortly," Susanne said smiling.

As Susanne left, the four played some more cards as they really didn't want to leave. Their legs were jelly, their bellies were full, and they were having fun playing cards. They eventually paid their bill, gathered their things, thanked Susanne, and said goodbye to the elderly couple sitting next to them. It was a memorable afternoon as they did the simple loop back to the parking lot, passing back down the valley through the tall evergreen forest.

By the time they got to the parking lot, the four weary travellers were exhausted. Thom welcomed the upcoming drive back into town. Charlotte kept complaining about blisters, while Bella complained about feeling her heartbeat in her fingers and toes.

Lacy was in terrific shape; she was tired but able to shoulder the aches and pains of the 15-mile hike.

Thom and Lacy shared a kiss behind the trunk latch once Charlotte and Bella were facing forward in the backseat and couldn't hear their conversation.

"I had such a great day. The girls loved it," Thom said.

"I had a super fun time too," Lacy smiled at Thom. "You might start missing this place when you're back in Toronto. You're going to be in such great shape too."

"I'll tell you; I can't remember falling asleep so quickly and sleeping so deeply as I have this past week," Thom said.

"Want to get out of here?" Lacy asked.

"Yes, I do," Thom said, as they both got in the car.

On the road back into Banff, Charlotte and Bella fell asleep almost immediately. Lacy placed her hand on top of Thom's on the shared armrest. Thom then turned and smiled at his co-pilot and navigator and interlocked his fingers with hers as the sun peeked behind the golden-hued horizon.

Chapter 11 - Lake Minnewanka

Charlotte and Bella woke the next morning feeling sore, but the good kind. Bella opened her eyes and the first thing she saw was the dream catcher that hung on the bedpost beside her nightstand. She reached out and stroked the feathers and reflected on the day before, swimming in the frigid Lake Annette, hiking 15 miles and having tea at the cabin in the woods. She thought about how clear her head was and how she was able to focus. Bella was truly hoping to see Brody this morning at breakfast so she could tell him about the previous day.

Charlotte woke soon after and let out a colossal moan as she stretched. "Whoa, my legs are sore."

"Mine too," Bella said as they both stared at the ceiling.

"I had the best dream. Me and you were driving in a convertible and driving through the mountains like Thelma and Louise," Charlotte said smiling.

"Sounds neat. Where were we going?" Bella asked.

"I don't remember, but I don't think it really mattered. We were in an old classic car, wearing sun dresses, sunglasses, and had handkerchiefs in our hair. What do you think it means?"

"Maybe we're destined to drive a car off a cliff," Bella joked.

Charlotte laughed. "I can't remember having a dream that clear and vivid."

"I've been sleeping deep myself. I think, maybe, I've been tossing and turning throughout the night, my entire life," Bella said as she got out of bed and went toward the bathroom.

"Hey girls, I'm going downstairs for breakfast! Come meet me soon!" Thom yelled from the other room.

"Ok dad. Be right down!" Charlotte yelled.

Both girls had never really felt this energized and motivated this early in the morning. It was usually a struggle, especially over the past 18 months. They didn't wake up and immediately feel sorry for themselves; they woke up with the feeling that this was going to be the best day of their lives.

Brody was working the breakfast shift and in the middle of preparing the restaurant for the day ahead. He was making coffee, pouring milks and creamers, and rolling silverware up in napkins. It was a moderately busy morning which gave him time to clean and polish surfaces throughout the kitchen, bar, and pass. He enjoyed mornings like this; he didn't feel like he was in the weeds, he had control over his tempo and emotions, he wasn't sweating, and he could work at his own pace.

Thom came into the dining room and sat at a table with the morning paper he had grabbed from the lobby. Brody immediately came over to him with a fresh pot of coffee.

"You read my mind, Brody," Thom said.

"You know it," Brody said.

"I'm gonna recommend you for the medal of honour, Brody," Thom joked.

"Thanks, Mr. Hudson. So, any big plans today?" Brody asked.

"I think we're going to try and figure that out," Thom said as he unfolded the paper.

"I was talking to my dad last night about going to Lake Minnewanka tomorrow, if you three want to come?" Brody suggested.

"I've heard of Lake Minnewanka, but I've never been," Thom said.

"We're planning on camping at Aylmer Junction and doing some fishing, hiking, and hopefully eating some BBQ lake trout for dinner," Brody said smiling.

"That sounds like a lot of fun. Your dad wouldn't mind?" Thom asked. "It's not like a father/son trip?"

"No, no, we talked about it. He thought it would be great if you and Bella and Charlotte came along," he said reassuringly. "We go out camping all the time."

"When the girls come down, I'll see what they say. But that sounds like a great plan," Thom said.

Brody walked back into the kitchen to drop some dirty dishes off. As he entered the kitchen, both the girls came into the dining room and sat down at the table with their father.

"Good morning, Pops," Charlotte said with a smile.

"Good morning, indeed," Thom said and smiled back at Charlotte and Bella.

"Is Brody working?" Bella immediately inquired.

"Yes, and he mentioned something I thought you two would find fun and interesting," Thom said.

"For God's sake, spit it out," Bella said jokingly.

Thom understood her dark humour. "Brody and his dad are going camping tomorrow on Lake Minnewanka and have invited us along for the adventure."

"And what did you say?" Bella impatiently asked.

"I said you probably wouldn't be interested," Thom replied.

"You said what?!" she gasped.

"Just kidding, I said I'd pass it by you two first," Thom said.

Charlotte got a kick out of this. "I love fishing. That sounds so fun."

"Dad, you almost gave me a heart attack," Bella said, holding her heart.

"So, you both want to go?" Thom asked.

"Yes!" Bella said, raising her voice by an octave.

Lacy was hard at work at the Banff Town Hall. She was typing proposals and reviewing budgets and permits of numerous projects that needed to be completed by the October deadline. The construction season in Banff was dictated by the weather, especially in the fall, when things were completely unpredictable. Most organizations like to have everything built by September, to avoid any potential disasters. She didn't mind the pressure at work, at all. She welcomed it, as winter was generally a slow time of year.

Suddenly, her office phone rang.

"Hello," she said.

"Hi, it's Thom."

"Well, how are you?" she said.

"I'm good. How about you?"

"I'm swell. Pretty busy though. What are you up to?" Lacy asked.

"Just up in my room. So, I don't want to keep you, but Jim Hughes, the lodge-owner and his son have invited us to go fishing on Lake Minnewanka tomorrow. I was thinking maybe you'd like to come along," Thom suggested.

"I haven't been to Lake Minnewanka in a long time. That place is so beautiful. I'd love to go," Lacy said.

Thom was relieved she agreed. "I was thinking of maybe booking a campsite at one of the spots on the lake. But there is just one thing…Me and the girls don't have a lot of camping gear."

"Well, you're in luck. I have plenty of gear; a couple of tents, extra sleeping bags, everything you could possibly need," Lacy said.

"I was thinking, why not make it a party and invite the whole gang?" Thom mentioned.

"Like Barb, Tammy, and the boys?" Lacy inquired. "Is Jim okay with that many people?"

"Yep. I passed it by him already. He said, 'more the merrier'. Invite them all: Pete, Jeff, Rob, Barb, and Tammy. I'll pay for two neighbouring sites," Thom suggested.

"That could be really fun. Let me pass it by everyone. Call me back in an hour," Lacy said.

"Sounds great, talk to you soon," Thom said.

"Ok, bye," Lacy said as she hung up the phone. There was a knock on her office door. "Come in."

Barb and Tammy stuck their heads inside the doorway.

"Good time?" Tammy asked.

"Yeah, come in. You're just the people I wanted to talk to," Lacy said. "Want to go camping at Lake Minnewanka tomorrow night?"

"That sounds fun," Barb said.

"I could do that," Tammy added.

"Perfect, do you think Jeff, Robby, and Pete will want to go?"

"Count them in," Barb immediately vouched for them.

There was another knock at Lacy's door.

"Come in," Lacy shouted.

Rob stuck his head in the door. "Secret meeting?"

"You, Jeff, and Pete are coming camping tomorrow night at Lake Minnewanka," Tammy commanded.

"Ok, sounds good," Rob said and left abruptly.

"That didn't take much convincing," Lacy said as all three shared a laugh.

Bella and Charlotte were watching some T.V. when their phone rang.

"Hello?" Bella answered.

"Hi, is Charlotte there?"

"Yes, may I ask who's calling?" Bella drilled.

"It's Zach. Is this Bella?"

"Yeah, hey Zach."

Charlotte immediately perked up and stared at Bella.

"So, did you have a good time at the Rose and Crown a couple nights ago?" Zach asked.

"We all had a great time… Here's Charlotte," Bella said, as she handed the phone to her sister.

"Hi, Zach!" Charlotte said enthusiastically.

"What are you doing?" Zach asked.

"Just watching T.V., chilling. What are you doing?"

"Just on my break. I thought I'd give you a call. So, I had a great time the other night and was wondering if you want to hang out again?" Zach said shyly.

"I'd like that. I'd never been that drunk in my life," Charlotte said, embarrassingly.

"You didn't drink that much, did you?" he innocently asked.

"It was the tequila; full black-out."

"Yep, that will do it," Zach said.

"I think we might be going fishing and camping tomorrow at Lake Minnewanka," Charlotte said.

"That sounds super gnarly," Zach said.

"Let me ask my dad, and maybe you could come with us?" Charlotte suggested.

"Sweet. I'll call you later. Hopefully you'll have some good news," Zach said.

"Do you have camping gear?" she asked.

"Oh, hell yeah!" Zach said.

"Perfect, talk to you later," Charlotte said.

"Ciao!" Zach said as they both hung up the phone.

"Sounds like it's going to be a party tomorrow night," Bella joked.

The plans had been set: four vehicles, twelve campers, two sites and five tents. It had grown from a father/son fishing trip to a large group adventure deep into the wilderness. The group was going to travel as a convoy, so they could all arrive and hike together. Jim was excited to have such a big group coming along. Usually, it was just him and his son, now he would have a whole gang come along for some laughs and adventures.

The four vehicles and campers gathered out front of the lodge so they would all depart at the same time. They were chatting, introducing themselves, sipping on morning coffee, and discussing the terrain that lay in front of them.

The Aylmer Junction camping area was deep in the heart of grizzly bear country. Grizzly bears were a protected species in Banff and had thrived there for over 100 years. Jim was an expert hunter and experienced outdoorsman who had encountered grizzly bears before. He knew it was good to travel in large groups as well as to know all the proper precautions surrounding potential encounters with bears. He knew bears were generally most dangerous in early spring or late fall, so the chances were good they wouldn't meet any grumpy bears.

Jim also knew there were large packs of wolves that roamed Banff National Park. After near obliteration, wolves had returned to the park in the early 1980s and were flourishing. Wolves were naturally afraid of humans, but if a person found themselves off alone or stranded, a pack might take advantage of a certain situation. Jim knew the importance of staying together and for people not to go off trail alone.

Once they had all become familiar with one another, the envoy set off, fully equipped, and ready for adventure. Jim drove Brody and Bella, Thom drove Charlotte and Zach, Lacy drove Barb and Tammy, and Pete drove Jeff and Rob.

The forecast called for clear blue skies all day and all night, but as every Albertan knows, nice weather can change in 15 minutes without warning. They were all prepared. They had rain gear, separate food packs, paracord, tarps, dry packs, everything they could possibly need under any condition. Jim brought bear spray, a shotgun, and a whistle; he knew the group probably wouldn't encounter any wolves or bears, but it was better to be prepared than not.

Jeff, Rob, and Pete were excited about the adventure. They brought in a propane stove, and enough food to feed a small army. It had been a while since the three guys had gone on an overnight. Barb and Tammy were just as excited to get out camping as the guys. Tammy had grown up in Revelstoke, B.C. and Barb grew up in Golden, B.C., so both ladies were used to hiking rough terrain and dealing with the dangers of nature.

The plan was to hike from the parking lot along the Lake Minnewanka trail, over the Stewart Canyon Bridge and then to the Alymer Pass Campground. They would then set up camp and hike up to the Aylmer Lookout and be back at camp before dinner.

The Bankhead parking lot was only a short drive from the village of Banff. Once they all arrived, they unpacked their gear from the vehicles and got a speech from Jim:

"Lake Minnewanka has had visitors for thousands of generations. Black bears and grizzlies have been coming down to drink the waters, fish the rivers, and eat the wild berries. We are a dozen people, all bears and wolves should hear us coming, I'm not too worried about that. What I am worried about is you wandering off alone. They suggest that anywhere you go, travel in groups of at least four people. Grizzly bears are 900 lbs, some are seven to eight feet long, they are terrific swimmers and climbers, and they also have a 975-psi biting capacity. They can bite clean through one of your arms or legs. Make noise when travelling; if you do come up on a grizzly, and you startle him, don't run, walk backwards without turning your back to him and get to a safe distance. Both Brody and I are carrying bear spray, and I have a shotgun for emergency protection. I truly don't suspect to encounter any bears, but please stick together and don't wander off alone. When we get to the site, I'll teach you how to keep yourself safe at night. Now, if you're all set, we'll get moving." Jim taught all of them something in this speech.

Bella turned to Charlotte. "So, you want me to back away from a charging bear?" she whispered to Charlotte.

"Stop being a baby," Charlotte said.

"900 pounds of flesh-eating carnivore," Bella persisted. "And you want me to stay calm?"

"Stop," Charlotte said. "Everything is going to be fine. Relax."

Jim led the entourage, followed by Thom and Lacy. Thom admired Jim; he ran a successful business, was a passionate cook, a devoted husband and father, and a modern-day Davy Crockett.

"This lake has been dammed on three different occasions, the final one, submerging a small town under 30 metres of glacier water," Jim said, giving them the full tour. "The lake is about 20 miles or 30 kilometres long and about 150 metres or 500 feet at its deepest point."

All the hikers looked out to the docks nearest to the parking area and saw a group getting their scuba gear ready to explore the underwater ghost town. They also saw several boats, including a Lake Minnewanka tour boat. It was a massive lake, darker in colour than that of Lake Louise's fluorescence, but still a striking blue-green hue.

"People love scuba diving here. That whole underwater town is perfectly preserved because of the cold water; hardly any decay," Jim continued.

The group passed several buildings including a restaurant, a bait shack, public washrooms and a picnic area with plenty of people enjoying the beautiful scenery and summer weather. After about 15 minutes, they had left any trace of human civilization and were amidst the evergreens.

The walk was pleasant, as the cool mountain breeze helped to keep everyone comfortable. The group came to the edge of the Cascade River, which was a glacial fed, shallow river that poured directly into Lake Minnewanka. They followed the river path atop the ravine for a few kilometres until they came to a rickety old wooden bridge that spanned across the river.

"This doesn't seem sketchy at all," Charlotte nervously joked.

"This is the Stewart Canyon Bridge, which crosses the Cascade River," Jim said to everyone. "It may look dangerous, but have no fear, park engineers assess this bridge every year, so it is perfectly safe." He turned to address the entire group. "We'll take the bridge across and take a short break by the sign on the other side."

Bella and Charlotte were nervous, but once they saw the group proceed without incident, it boosted their confidence. The girls even stopped halfway to take a few pictures with their Pentax cameras.

"I can't believe the water is so clear," Charlotte said.

"It's nothing like the Don River, eh?" Bella replied.

"This is how beer commercials are conceived," Zach joked.

The twelve hikers moved across the bridge and gathered by the Stewart Canyon Bridge sign. They off-loaded their heavy packs, hydrated, ate some snacks, and sat down on a few downed trees and regained their breath.

"Pete, you look winded. We are just getting started," Jeff poked fun at Pete.

"Can you carry me?" Pete said like a child.

"Are we there yet?" Rob added for good measure.

Though it had only been about an hour of hiking, the gear they were carrying made it seem much longer. Thom wiped his sweaty head with a handkerchief and pondered the remaining time in Banff before heading back to Ontario in a few days' time. He turned to Lacy and gave her a big smile. "How are you making out?" he asked.

"Doing great. How about you? Pretty heavy pack, eh?" Lacy observed.

"Yeah, this tent is a killer," he said thinking about Lacy's kindness and beauty.

"Do you want some of my granola bar?" Lacy offered.

"No thanks," Thom said with a smile.

After a few minutes, Jim once again addressed the group: "Alright folks, ready to get moving? We have about an hour left until we make the camping spot, and luckily it is mostly flat terrain," he said, flinging his pack over his shoulder.

The group regeared and started back along the path into the evergreen forest. After a few minutes, they came to an outcropping that looked down on Lake Minnewanka. The sun's rays poked through the clouds and cast down on the blue waters.

"I think I'm having a religious moment," Rob joked as everyone laughed.

"That is something," Barb added.

"Yeah, something out of the Bible," Tammy added.

Clouds were starting to roll in over the mountains, but it was still a sunny beautiful day. Jim took notice, but nobody else paid attention to the shifting conditions. He turned back and looked west to check the horizon to see if there were any systems creeping in.

"What is it, Dad?" Brody asked.

"Nothing," Jim said, as they continued down the path.

The group pressed on through the pristine wilderness. They caught glimpses of elk and a white-tailed deer along the distant shoreline and a herd of mountain goats as they scaled the cliffs above. The path narrowed the further they went and eventually declined back down to Lake Minnewanka and opened to a few campsites at the water's edge. Bella's anxiety skyrocketed as she kept noticing the grizzly bear warning signs. Brody noticed her look of concern and instantly tried to reassure her of safety. "Don't worry," he said, "I've camped here for years and never had any bear problems."

"That didn't help at all," Bella quipped.

"As long as we're making noise, moving in groups and equipped with bear spray, we'll be good." Brody doubled down on his assurance.

"What if the bear comes at night and pulls us out of the tent by our feet?" Zach joked.

Charlotte punched him hard in the arm. "Stop," she said, "Bella has crippling anxiety, and we left her meds at the lodge."

"Not funny, Charlotte," Bella said.

Jim led the hikers to the campsites. "Here we are folks! Let's try and keep our tents close together with the doors facing one another. We'll keep the cooking area near the shore and away from the tents."

It was a perfect spot, Thom thought. His architectural brain was always thinking about unique and creative spots for homes, and this would be the ultimate location. The campsite had a large, rocky beach, a gorgeous view of the lake, and a picturesque mountain backdrop.

"What do you think, Thom?" Jim asked.

"I've never seen a campsite like it," he responded.

"It's like something out of a dream, isn't it?" Jim said as he looked out over the lake. "This lake is two or three million years old. The Stoney Nakoda people called it Minn-wake, or the 'Lake of the Spirits,' because they believed it contained evil spirits. For thousands of years, they both feared and respected its might."

"Amazing," Thom said, looking out on the lake.

"To think that the Nakoda have been fishing here for 10,000 years is remarkable," Jim said.

The group got busy setting up camp. Barb and Tammy set up their dome tent with relative ease, while Jeff, Rob, and Pete kept on micro-managing each other, so they took a little longer to set up. Zach, Charlotte, Brody, and Bella set up their huge four-person tent and Lacy and Thom set up their little tent. Jim set up a little pitch-tent that took him 45 seconds. After that, he took out his fishing rod and gear and headed to the lake side.

"Coming Brody?" Jim yelled to his son from the shoreline.

"Yeppers! Just a couple of minutes!" Brody yelled back.

Bella turned to Brody. "You're leaving me alone in grizzly bear territory?"

"I'll just be down there," he said with a smile. "Don't worry, you have Charlotte to protect you."

"I'll make sure she covers herself with barbeque sauce and keeps an apple in her mouth at all times," Zach joked.

"You are not funny, sir," Bella told Zach.

Barb, Tammy, Jeff, Rob, and Pete set up the cooking area. They brought a couple of large wooden picnic tables together, set up the propane stove, and started a small fire in the nearby fire pit. Tammy had brought a couple of red and white checkered plastic tablecloths that she spread out. The co-workers were excellent as a team. Jeff started cooking bacon on the propane stove, Pete chopped some wood for the night, Barb and Tammy started making sandwiches and snacks, while Rob dragged logs into place around the campfire, so everyone would be able to sit down together.

Brody joined his father fishing at the lakeshore. It had been a couple months since they had a day off together and were able to dip their lines in. Brody wanted to catch a few fish too, not only to impress Bella, but to eat as well. Brody loved the passive nature of fishing and the excitement of landing a fighting fish. Jim had shown Brody everything he knew about angling and considered his son to be a great fisherman.

"Any bites?" Brody asked his dad.

"Nothing yet," Jim responded. "I think we'll head down shore, where there's that sharp drop-off. We should be able to nail a couple of those suckers."

Lacy and Thom watched as Jim and Brody walked and cast their lines and slowly made their way down the shoreline.

"Brody seems like such a decent kid," Lacy said to Thom as he blew up an air mattress.

"He's a stand-up kid. Bella really has a thing for him."

"Well, he does seem as if he's got his stuff together," Lacy said.

"Yeah, we know where she gets that from," Thom joked as he finished blowing up the mattress.

"You're pretty funny," Lacy laughed. "It's probably going to be hard on them when you leave."

"I'm sure they are going to remain in close contact." Thom threw the mattress inside the tent. "Bella said she was even going to sign up for an email account," Thom said. "Same goes for Zach and Charlotte." He then sat on a nearby log and Lacy sat down beside him. "It is pretty remarkable that all three of us met some new friends on this vacation."

"Sounds like you just needed a change of scenery. Like a slumping ballplayer getting traded to a new team," Lacy said.

"Now all three of us are on hitting streaks!" Thom said. "Honestly, Lacy, this has been such a great trip. So rewarding; meeting you, seeing the girls so happy, all the adventures and beautiful weather we've been having. I wish it would never end."

Lacy smiled at Thom's genuine honesty, leaned in, and gave him a kiss on the cheek. "You are a pretty special guy yourself and you deserve the absolute best," she said.

Thom turned and looked at Lacy. "Thanks, Lacy. That means so much. You deserve the absolute best, as well."

Bella and Charlotte sat down beside Barb and Tammy playing cards at one of the picnic tables. Barb and Tammy both turned to the newcomers with interest.

"Challenge!" Bella proposed.

"Want to play euchre?" Charlotte asked the two ladies.

"Sure thing. You two versus us two?" Tammy challenged.

"Bring it on," Charlotte said.

The four girls were perfectly content to sit, while Jeff, Rob, and Pete continued to do the work. Pete threw some bread to toast atop the grill over the fire, while Rob and Jeff prepared the rest of the B.L.T. fixings.

Zach had changed into his bathing suit and sprinted into the frigid waters. He let out a wild yelp as everyone turned to see the commotion.

"That kid is crazy," Lacy said.

"He's surprisingly got a lot in common with Charlotte," Thom raised his eyebrows at the thought.

"Hey kiddos, BLTs are ready for anyone who wants one!" Jeff shouted.

Everyone sat at the picnic table and had BLTs, chips, veggies, and dip for lunch. Pete kept toasting bread, and Jeff kept assembling the sandwiches. They were all very quiet, which was a clear sign that they were all hungry after such a long hike.

"Great job guys!" Barb said to Jeff, Rob, and Pete.

"Soooo good," Lacy added. "Just what I needed."

As the group was finishing lunch, Jim and Brody came from down the shoreline, each carrying two massive lake trout. Everyone looked at the fisherman with smiles, especially Bella who couldn't help but be proud of him and what a great worker he was.

"A good catch!" Thom yelled.

"Didn't take long at all," Jim yelled back.

Thom turned to Lacy. "They were only gone for an hour."

"So, do you two want a B.L.T.?" Jeff asked the fishermen.

"Is there some left?" Brody asked as he dropped his fish near the water's edge. "I'm starving."

"Lots left," Pete said.

Jim knelt to the fish at the water's edge. He opened his fishing bag and began processing the large trout. "I'm going to hold off until dinner. Thanks anyways," he said. "I'm going to make up some delicious appetizers."

Thom was shocked at Jim's ability to fillet a fish. Obviously, he was a chef and had done it before, but he worked at an incredible speed with phenomenal precision. Jim threw the fish guts into the water and ziplocked the trout fillets and put them in the nearby cooler.

Everyone finished up their sandwiches and burned their paper plates in the fire. Tammy wiped down the table, while Barb did her best to put everything away.

"Wanna play some more cards?" Charlotte asked Barb and Tammy as they were cleaning.

"Sounds good," Tammy said.

"Fine by me," Barb added.

"Does anyone still want to make the climb up to the Aylmer Pass Lookout?" Thom asked.

"I'm in," Zach said.

"I'm in too," Brody said.

Everyone nodded at one another in agreement.

"Ok, you see those brown lockers over there," Jim said as he pointed to the lockers about 50 metres from the campsite. "These are for food storage. At night and when we are away from the site, we're going to store all our food in those containers." The containers were large enough for the coolers and bags and were certainly bear-proof, as they were made of plate steel and had a 12-inch concrete foundation. Dinosaurs would have trouble getting in there.

Everyone did their share to help clean up. A short while later, the entire group would start the climb up Aylmer Valley. It was a steep climb over the sandstone and shale terrain, and everyone needed to be wary of their footing. It was easy not paying attention and twist an ankle or buckle one's knee. They made their way through the aspen grove lining the shoreline and up into the spruce, pine, and hemlock forest that became sparser the higher they climbed. The trail thinned after around 20 minutes of hiking and the group passed into rocky meadows of wildflowers. The entire landscape was in full bloom with varieties of wild rose and strawberry, rock jasmine, fire weed, yellow columbine, and heart-leaved arnica.

The sun beat down on the swaying fields and everyone took notice of how the mountain seemed alive. The higher they got, the thinner the air and cooler the breeze. Clouds were now getting a bit thicker, but it was still a beautiful day. This hike was more on the challenging side, as inclines were steep and there were few switchbacks. The group moved in single file through the colourful meadows until they reached the peak of Aylmer Lookout. The Aylmer Mountain summit was much higher than the lookout, but the group had already hiked most of the day and were not equipped to scale the treacherous terrain to the top.

Aylmer Lookout was a spectacle to behold. The group looked down onto Lake Minnewanka which looked like a polished gem from their vantage point. It truly gave the group perspective on how long the lake was as it wrapped around Mount Girouard on the opposite side of the lake. A single boat carved through the middle of the lake and created a wake with perfect symmetry. It almost appeared like a plane in the sky.

Bella, Charlotte, Zach, and Brody all sat down, side-by-side on a nearby boulder and took in the scenery together.

"Do you see our camp down there?" Brody said, pointing down below.

"I think I do," Bella said.

"I'm having so much fun with you guys," Zach said in a very soft-spoken voice.

"Thanks, Zach," Charlotte said. "I'm having the time of my life out here with you guys, too."

"Honestly, the best moment of my life, so far," Zach said as he put his arm around Charlotte.

"You're the best," Charlotte turned and kissed him on the cheek, and he pretended to faint and fall backwards onto the rock.

"It's probably one of the best moments in my life too," Bella said.

Brody put his arm around Bella and squeezed her tight. "Me too," he said.

The four young adults sat looking and soaking in all the details of the landscape; the various treelines on distant mountains, the river systems, the clouds that rolled over the range and sun that shone on their faces. The novelty of hiking these mountains was not wearing thin for Bella and Charlotte. Their bodies seemed completely in tune with their minds and soul.

After a short rest, the group made their way back down the mountain; down the meadows, through the evergreen forest and eventually into the aspen grove that was at water's level. Once they reached the camp, everyone seemed to retreat into their tents for a little afternoon nap. It was certainly earned.

Around an hour later, people began to stir again as their bellies moaned. Pete re-stoked the fire, Jim prepared the fresh trout fillets with spices and lemon, Rob wrapped baked potatoes, and Jeff started to chop vegetables. Tammy, Barb, and Lacy helped to set the table. Lacy brought out two whole chickens that she butterfly cut, spiced, and put on the grill. Thom added a couple bottles of red wine to accompany the feast to come.

After about an hour of cooking and preparing, the group sat down for a delicious, memorable feast of trout, chicken, baked potatoes, carrots, broccoli, and cauliflower. After such a long day, the food tasted as if was cooked at a five-star restaurant. Everyone complimented each other on their different dishes, especially Jim and Brody's freshly caught trout. They laughed and shared stories about tourists, different adventures, work projects, and future plans. Everyone got along so well, it made teamwork and cleanup a breeze. Before long the sun was going down and thicker clouds began to roll into camp.

Once the food was put back in the locker and the cleanup was done, everyone got into warmer gear and huddled by the fire that was freshly stoked and burning bright. The temperature had dropped significantly since the sun disappeared behind the mountains.

Jim began with a story. "Since around the 1850's, reports began surfacing of a large creature that was spotted along Minnewanka's shoreline." Jim paused and pointed out across the lake. "Speaking with the Nakota elders, they spoke about some gargantuan 19-inch footprints, bigger than a bear's, and hair-raising screams from the locals. Sightings of enormous hairy beasts began flooding the local press and the legend of the Lake Minnewanka Wildman was born. In 1899, an Irishman reported shooting it several times as the beast stalked his horses and the very last time it was seen, a short while later, was when a man on horseback saw it limping off to the west, perhaps to find a place with fewer people."

Everyone pretended not to be scared, but it was a terrifying story, considering they were all alone in the middle of the Rocky Mountains in the pitch-black dark. The thought of bears crept back into the minds of all the campers.

"An elder of the Stoney people was the first person to lay eyes on the body of water from the summit of one of the highest mountains overlooking the lake." Jim pointed to various mountain peaks. "From his elevated vantage point, the man noticed a fish that appeared to be as long as the lake, leading him to call the lake, "Lake of the Evil Water Spirit." The Stoney people both respected and feared the lake for its resident spirits." Jim paused while everyone whispered with one another. "One of those spirits speaks of a mythical half-man, half-fish creature that once lived here in Minnewanka. It had sunken dark eyes with razor sharp teeth, skinny pale arms with claw-like fingernails. The grotesque merman struck fear and panic in all those who saw it swimming in the emerald water before it was allegedly captured."

Charlotte and Bella had heard ghost stories before, but the stories Jim told made them genuinely afraid. A lot of the fear came from being scared of wolves and grizzly bears, but the darkness of the night and the coolness of the foggy air made them stay extra close to the fire and each other.

As the group enjoyed the fire, roasted marshmallows, chatted, and shared stories, rain began to trickle down.

"Anyone else feel that?" Jeff asked as he raised his hand to test the incoming droplets.

"Starting to come down," Rob added.

The group started to hear the sizzles as the rain pellets hit the fire.

"I think we better batten down the hatches," Thom said.

"Ok, everyone, don't leave anything outside that you don't want getting wet," Jim announced.

"Well, it was good while it lasted," Barb added as she and Tammy went to their tent.

"Ok, see everyone in the morning," Lacy said, as she and Thom went to their tent.

The four teens, Zach, Charlotte, Bella, and Brody went to their tent, Jeff, Rob, and Pete went to their enormous canvas tent and the last person to go to their tent was Jim. He browsed the site scanning for any potential danger or food that may have been left out. Once he did a lap of the campsite, he crawled into his modest tent and lay down for the night.

Everyone was exhausted. The day had been packed with an early rise, a car ride, a long hike with heavy gear, setting up camp, cooking meals, and another long, steep hike. Bella and Charlotte were happy to snuggle up next to Brody and Zach. All four of them knew it was not only awkward, but tactless to make-out lying next to each other. They shared some small talk, but realized they were all too exhausted to try and hold out any longer. Before long, they were sound asleep.

Tammy and Barb chatted away and did some reading under their small, battery-powered lantern, while Jeff, Rob, and Pete played some cards in their tent. Eventually all of them gave way to their weariness and passed out.

Lacy and Thom were happy to get some private time together and shared some intimacy, however, their nightly neighbours were only feet away, so they showed restraint and tact as they slowly drifted into dreamland.

Jim set his bear spray and loaded 20-gauge by the foot of his bed near the door-zipper. He knew, if bears were to come around, it would be at night. He ran through the checklist in his head as he lay down and closed his eyes. Before long, he drifted off to sleep.

Deep into the night, the rain had let up and silence fell over the camp. Only distant drips from treetops could be heard as they fell upon the tent tops. Bella tossed in her sleep and as she rolled over onto her back, she opened her eyes in confusion. She didn't know where she was. She looked to her side to see Charlotte and remembered they were camping. Right, Lake Minnewanka she thought. It was eerily quiet, except for the occasional rain drop above her. She then heard a twig snap about 10 metres from her tent. She immediately froze as her eyes strained in shock. Her adrenaline kicked in and she could hardly move. She slowly turned to see Brody sound asleep as another twig snapped in the distance. Her heart skipped a beat as she was paralyzed with fear. She knew whatever was out there was getting closer to the tent. A moment later, she heard what sounded like a dog sniffing right outside the tent by her feet and saw a giant shadow pass as another stick snapped. Its loud, heavy footsteps were so close she could feel them in her bed.

Bella gave Charlotte a nudge, but she simply rolled away from her and gave a disgruntled moan. She could hear the animal huffing and breathing heavily as it seemed to move toward the firepit. The fire had long gone out, so it was pitch-black outside. Bella wondered if anyone else was awake, but she didn't want to make any noise for fear of being dragged out by her feet and eaten alive.

Bella then heard the animal enter water and couldn't help but think of the Minnewanka Wildman and the Merman stories that Jim had told around the campfire. She could hear her heart beating as the animal continued to move in the water just metres from her tent. She could hear the animal chewing and crunching on bones and realized it could be eating the fish scraps that were discarded in the water by Jim and Brody earlier in the day.

The beast slowly moved out of the water and appeared to be approaching her tent again. From across the camp, Bella heard someone yell: "Hey, bear!" The bear gave a loud roar. She heard another "Hey, bear!" Bella clenched her teeth and the rest of her body as she lay silent. She prayed the beast would just run off. There was a sound of spraying and then a sound of galloping. Bang went the first shot and the bear's footsteps continued. Two more shots; bang, bang. The blasts of gun were so loud Bella grasped her ears as everyone in her tent sprung from their deep sleep. She heard a grunt from the beast as it seemed to have fallen to the forest floor. Finally, there was a large exhale from the bear and then silence.

"It's okay, everyone!" Jim shouted. "You can come out."

Everyone slowly trickled out of their tents to see Jim kneeling just a few feet from an enormous grizzly bear carcass. He held his smoking shotgun with his head hung down.

"He wouldn't scare. He charged and I shot," Jim said, as everyone stood in shock watching the carcass steaming.

"Are you alright, Dad?" Brody asked.

"Took three rounds, almost point-blank range. He finally dropped about six feet from me," Jim said, obviously rattled by the experience.

"Jesus Christ," Jeff said.

"Holy smokes!" Pete said, coming out of the tent seeing the dead bear laying on the ground.

"Thank God," Thom said.

Bella was the last to emerge from the tents. She was shaking, but relieved to see the beast was no more. She noticed the toxic smell of bear spray and gunpowder in the air as her anxiety slowly released. She was shocked by the size of it. Brody put her arm around her and pulled her in close.

Everyone was at a loss for words until Thom broke the silence: "Thank God you brought what you did, Jim."

"I left the fish scraps too shallow and too close to camp," Jim responded, shaking his head.

"Definitely not your fault. This bear was clearly mean and agitated," Brody said, supporting his Dad.

"A young dumb, juvenile male, playing tough," Jim said, still shaking his head.

"I heard the bear coming, I heard it breathing. I froze, I was completely locked up," Bella said.

"Understandable, Bella," Tammy said. "I think I urinated in my pants."

Thom consoled his frightened young daughter as everyone just looked on with shock and amazement. "You're okay now, Bella."

It took some time for everyone to process what had happened. Most of the campers were so tired that they trickled back into the tents and would deal with the aftermath in the morning. Jim made sure everyone was feeling alright before they went back to bed. Thom was the last camper up with Jim.

"Could you help me out for a few minutes?" Jim asked.

"Sure, no problem," Thom answered. "What's this all about?"

Jim handed Thom a knife, smiled and said, "You'll see."

Chapter 12 - The Last Supper

B rody's mother Allison was helping to clean and set the dining room tables for dinner service at the lodge. There was only one lone man drinking coffee watching the news on the small television behind the bar. Allison hadn't heard any news from Brody and Jim, let alone anything about a grizzly bear coming into their camp in the middle of the night. She had no reason to worry. Jim and Allison had been on many adventures together and encountered several bears throughout the years. They had been to Alaska, the Yukon, and many other remote places in the world. Most bears did not want anything to do with humans. The only time they became aggressive was when they were starving, or it was a mother defending her cubs. Allison knew Jim could protect himself and the others with his skills and knowledge.

The restaurant phone rang, and Allison picked it up at the end of the bar where the lone man was sitting. "Hello?" she answered.

"Hey honey, it's me." It was Jim on the line.

"So, how was camping? Where are you?" Allison asked.

"We're just leaving Minnewanka now. I need you to make a reservation for 12 people later tonight around 7 o'clock. We're gonna have some guests."

"Babe, what's wrong? You don't sound good," Allison said.

"Everything's fine. Certainly have some interesting stories to tell. Listen, we're going to have a dinner party tonight. Me, you,

Brody, Thom, his girls, and a few other friends. Is there a lot on the books?"

"Only a couple of four tops," Allison answered as she looked at the reservation book.

"Perfect, Mark and Suzy should be able to handle things. I'll be there in a couple hours. I'm gonna go home and get cleaned up first. I'll see you soon," Jim said.

"Ok, babe. See you soon," Allison hung up the phone with a look of concern.

"Everything alright?" the old man asked as he took a sip of coffee.

"I don't know, he wouldn't say," Allison said. "Do you want some more coffee?"

"You bet."

"Something must have happened at Minnewanka." Allison thought out loud.

"Maybe it was the Wildman or maybe the half fish, half man," The old man suggested.

"Very funny," she said.

Once all the campers got back to the parking lot, they went their separate ways. It had been a crazy night, especially for Bella, who was fairly upset by the incident, but feeling better after a few hours of sleep. The hike back through the woods and over the Stewart Canyon was, in some ways, soothing for everyone. It gave, not only Bella, but each hiker a chance to reflect and feel normal again.

Jim drove Zach and Brody in his truck; Lacy dropped Thom, Bella, and Charlotte off at the lodge and Jeff, Pete, and Rob left at the same time as Barb and Tammy. They all certainly had stories to tell. Everyone had one thing on their minds: have a hot shower and get into fresh clothes.

Once Thom, Bella, and Charlotte were back in their room at the lodge, Bella immediately jumped in the shower. It was an extra-long, hot, soothing shower which made her feel a thousand times better.

Charlotte banged on the bathroom door. "Come on, Bella. You're taking way too long!"

"Shut your cake hole," Bella yelled. "I'll be right out."

Thom was eager to shower but wasn't as impatient as Charlotte. He instead chose to step on the balcony and soak in the view. He thought about getting his firearms licence once he got back to Ontario. He thought about Jim's valiant actions and how if he hadn't been there, things might have gone drastically different. He was glad things turned out the way they did, and he kept telling himself not to be afraid of the wilderness. The bear had wandered into the camp, being led by its stomach, was caught off-guard and decided to defend itself and ended up paying the ultimate price for its decision.

Charlotte hopped into the shower and took just as long as Bella. The bear shooting was all a blur for Charlotte, but it still rattled her, the yelling, the gunshots and the huge steaming, wretched carcass. She thought to herself that if she ever went hiking deep in the valleys of the Rocky Mountains, she too would need to arm herself, something that never occurred to her while living in urban Toronto.

"There better be hot water left when I get in there!" Thom yelled.

"What!?" Charlotte yelled from the bathroom.

"I'm prettier than you!" Bella yelled back in a joking manner.

"What!?" she yelled again.

Thom turned back around to look at the mountains once again. He deeply reflected on the vacation they had enjoyed so far.

It was all enjoyable until three deafening shotgun rounds went off a few feet from his ears. Lacy, he thought, had been surprisingly calm about the whole ordeal. He was really falling for her. She was smart, they had similar interests, values, careers, and they truly enjoyed each other's company.

This was going to be their last night in Banff together, as he and the girls were on their way back to Calgary the following afternoon to catch the flight back to Toronto. He had never seen Bella and Charlotte so happy and having so much fun together. He saw so much of himself in his girls. They loved the Banff energy and culture as much as their parents. Thom's major goal was to show Bella and Charlotte where he and their mother met and first fell in love; the results were beyond successful. They had turned a major corner, they had met new friends, tried new things, and were full of positive energy.

"It's all yours, Dad!" Charlotte yelled from the other room, interrupting Thom's train of thought.

"Okay, sweetie," Thom yelled back.

Thom hopped in the shower and couldn't remember a shower ever feeling so great. It had been a long 24 hours; blood, sweat, and tears. The hot water helped to relieve tension in his neck and shoulders that had built up as the result of carrying a 50-pound backpack. He now realized why Bella and Charlotte had taken so long; he was having deep thoughts as the hot water beat down on his weary body. He would never take running hot water for granted again.

Charlotte knocked on the bathroom door. "Hey Dad, me and Bella are gonna go do a load of laundry."

"Okay, sweetie," Thom shouted.

When he came out of the steamy bathroom, the air seemed sweet as it poured in through the balcony door, cooling his core temperature. He got changed and laid down on his bed to have a short nap. He dozed off almost immediately.

Charlotte and Bella sat in the laundry room in the basement of the lodge. There were a few vending machines, a few sets of washing machines and dryers, as well as a cork board with a variety of posters and business cards pinned to it.

"All my clothes smell like campfire," Bella said.

"Same," Charlotte said as they both started the washing machines.

"So, are you excited to go home tomorrow?" Bella asked.

"Not really. I like this place," Charlotte said. "Now I know why Mom loved Banff so much."

"It does feel a lot more normal than Toronto," Bella reflected.

"It has great energy here. Everyone has been so nice," Charlotte added.

"I'm gonna miss Brody. We said we're going to talk every day, but obviously I'm going to miss his company," Bella said with a sad face.

"I've had a great time with Zach too. He said he's coming to Ontario in a few months to visit family. But who knows what is going to happen. He's so funny," Charlotte said with a smile. "We're gonna be okay, Bella."

"I know, it's just kind of sad." Bella frowned again.

"That bear last night was crazy, eh?" Charlotte asked.

"I'm glad I didn't move when I first heard him. He was sniffing right by our feet. I could hear him breathing, for God's sake," Bella recalled.

"Dad wants us to take the firearms training course together," Charlotte suggested.

"Damn straight," Bella affirmed.

Bella and Charlotte laughed together, and the tension eased as the day went by. They both sat down as the washing machines continued their cycles. The girls laughed and shared stories of the past couple of weeks; they talked about the uncertainty of their future; they talked about school, boys, their Dad and Lacy, and everything in between. Both Charlotte and Bella truly had a bonding moment in the lodge's laundry room.

Allison was setting the dining room table for 13 guests. Brody and Jim came through the kitchen doors into the dining room buttoning up their chef coats.

"Hey, Mom!" Brody said.

"Hey, sweetie," Allison said as she placed the last wine glass into place. "So, how was your adventure? Everything go okay?"

"Well, Dad had to take down a juvenile grizzly bear that wandered into camp," Brody said.

"I yelled at it, I sprayed it, I threatened it, nothing. Then it charged me, and I had to shoot it," Jim explained. "It should have known better, the poor thing."

"It was an aggressive adolescent male. Probably never seen a human before," Brody added.

"Jesus, that must have been scary for everyone," Allison said as she thought about Bella and Charlotte.

"Everyone was rattled. It was the middle of the night," Jim said. "Eventually everyone made it back to sleep, but God, what a rude awakening."

"Bella was wide awake when the bear came in," Brody explained. "She heard it walking, sniffing, and breathing all around the tent. I'm so glad Dad woke up when he did."

"Jesus. I'm glad you were there, hon," Allison said.

"I've never had an experience like it," Jim shook his head. "We've seen tons of bears in the wild. I must have spooked it really good."

"Ornery bear, eh?" Allison reflected.

"Yeah." There was a pause before Jim changed the conversation. "So, Brody and I are going to start preparing dinner for the party tonight. We want to make their last night in Banff super special."

"We're all set out here. Should be a slow night," Allison said as she started to fold napkins.

"Great," Jim said as he and Brody went back into the kitchen.

Thom awoke from his nap as Charlotte and Bella came back into the room carrying their freshly done laundry.

"Wakey, wakey," Charlotte said as Thom rubbed his eyes.

"Feel better?" Bella asked.

"That is exactly what I needed," Thom said as he sat up.

"You almost ready for dinner, Dad?" Bella reminded.

"Man, I'm starving," Thom said.

"You were out for a while," Bella added.

"Yeah, I must have needed it," Thom said. "They're expecting us in an hour. Maybe we should pack and get everything ready for tomorrow, so we don't have to worry about it in the morning."

Thom, Bella, and Charlotte packed their clothes, a few souvenirs and laid their dream catchers on top. The girls each reflected on their father's gift and its symbolic relevance as well as the powers that came from within. They promised themselves to hang the dream catchers wherever they went in life; they had certainly worked so far.

Allison was lighting candles throughout the dining room as Maggie polished glasses behind the bar. A delicious scent wafted from the kitchen and throughout the dining room as the sun set behind the mountains. Jeff, Pete, and Rob came in through the front doors dressed in nice shirts and dress pants. They were all in good spirits, as usual. All three men sat at the bar as Maggie smiled.

"Hi fellas. How's it going this evening?"

"I'd be a lot better with a dry vodka martini," Jeff said.

"Easy cowboy," Rob said to Jeff and turned to Maggie. "We are doing great, thanks. What's your name?"

"It's Maggie," she said with a coy smile.

"Maggie. Great. How are things with you?" Rob said.

"Pretty amazing, thanks," Maggie said. "Can I get you guys something?"

"Well, we all know Jeff would like a vodka crantini," Rob joked.

"Dry vodka martini, hold the cranberry, please," Jeff added.

"I'll have a rye and ginger ale, please," Rob asked.

"I'll have a pint of your finest, please," Pete asked.

"Sounds great," Maggie said as she started to prepare the drinks.

Allison led Tammy and Barb into the bar area where they joined the three guys.

"Well, howdy campers," Tammy joked.

"Hey Tammy. Hey Barb. Are you two doing alright?" Pete asked.

"Well, I had a two-and-a-half-hour shower, took a nap, and smoked a pack of cigarettes, so I'm doing fine," Barb joked as everyone laughed.

"I took a two-and-a-half-hour shower, had a nap, drank a bottle of wine, and took 3 Xanax, so I'm also doing fine," Tammy said as the group laughed.

"Can I get you ladies something?" Maggie asked as she shook the martini in the decanter.

"I'll have a vodka/soda please," Barb said.

"I'll do a gin and tonic, please," Tammy said.

"Sounds good," Maggie said as she poured the martini and put a sword with olives in the drink.

Zach came into the bar area carrying a present. "Hello, long time no see," he said to everyone in a joking manner.

"Hey bud," Pete said.

"Are you doing alright, kid?" Rob asked.

"Had a little myocardial infarction, nothing major," Zach said. "I'm glad Crocodile Dundee was with us though."

Everyone shared another laugh as the tension of the previous night was still fizzling.

"Can I grab you something?" Maggie asked Zach.

"Can I have a Coke, please?" Zach asked.

"No problem," Maggie said with a smile.

Thom, Bella, and Charlotte came into the dining room looking completely refreshed. Both Bella and Charlotte were wearing dresses and had put on makeup for their final dinner at the lodge. Zach couldn't believe his eyes. It was like seeing Charlotte in a whole new light. She smiled at the frozen Zach.

"Hi, you look terrific," Zach immediately told her.

"Thanks," she said.

"I bought you a little going away gift," he said, handing her the gift he brought.

"For me?" Charlotte said as she unwrapped the gift as everyone looked on.

"It's nothing special," Zach said shyly.

Charlotte opened the gift to find a keychain shaped like Canada with two hearts where Banff and Toronto would be, with the engraving '3500 km has nothing on us.' She smiled as she looked up to meet Zach's eyes. She hugged him and said: "Thank you, I love it."

"I'm glad. I had it specially made. Check the back," Zach said.

Tammy and Barb looked at each other and did the same 'ahh' face.

Charlotte flipped the keychain to see 'C + Z, July 1998'. "There's something else in the box," Zach said.

Charlotte reached inside and pulled out a CD. "Stoner Haze!" she yelled and hugged Zach again. "I love it!"

Jeff turned to Pete and Rob. "Must be a local band."

Brody and Jim came from the kitchen into the dining room to see almost the entire gang at the bar enjoying themselves. Thom immediately shook Jim's hand as they smiled at each other.

"It smells great in here," Thom said to Jim.

"We have a beautiful stew reduction and a roast in the oven," Jim said.

Brody hugged Bella immediately. "How are you doing?" he asked.

"Way better after the hot shower," Bella said.

"Tell me about it. Mine was at least 30 minutes," Brody said.

"Same," Bella said with a smile.

"You look absolutely lovely," Brody said as if he couldn't believe his eyes.

"Thank you," Bella said. "You're not so bad yourself."

"Oh, you're just saying that. I have a going away gift for you," Brody reached behind the bar and gave Bella a wrapped parcel.

"I have a gift for you too," Bella said as she handed him a small parcel. "You open yours first."

Brody opened the small box to reveal a small picture frame with a picture of them Bella had taken on Banff Avenue. "You got these pictures developed already?"

"Got them done a few days ago."

"I love it," Brody said as he couldn't take his eyes off the picture. "Open yours."

Bella ripped the paper off the parcel and opened the small box to reveal a necklace with a small horse charm on a silver chain. "It's so pretty."

"It's the Calgary Stampeder logo. Hopefully it reminds you of meeting up in Calgary, watching the football game and the fireworks that night," Brody said with a smile.

Bella remembered meeting at the Saddledome, the silly business with the mascot, holding hands and kissing under the Canada Day fireworks. Brody was so special to her. He was wise for his age, he was caring, kind, trustworthy, and hardworking. Brody was truly unlike any other boy she had ever met. "I love it!" Bella reached out and hugged Brody with all her might.

"A Stampeder necklace. Neat," Thom said overlooking his daughter's sweet little exchange, then turned his head to see Lacy come into the dining room, wearing a red dress that immediately struck Thom. At first, he felt completely out of her league. He checked himself; he wiped down his shirt, rolled his tongue along his teeth to check for food particles and subtly cleared his throat. He adored her, but this look elevated her to another level.

"Hi, Lacy. You look stunning," Thom said, hoping he didn't sound ridiculous.

"Yourself as well," Lacy said with a smile.

"I'm so glad you're here."

"I wouldn't miss it," Lacy said sincerely.

It had only been a few hours since they all left one another, but everyone felt like they hadn't seen each other for some time.

They all felt a thousand times better than earlier in the day. They mingled, smiled, shared stories, and chatted at the bar over cocktails and wine while the food simmered to completion.

"If everyone would like to make their way over to the table; appetizers will be served momentarily," Jim said as everyone listened and started to move over to the impressively set table.

There were wine glasses, water glasses, five pieces of silverware per setting, fancy folded napkins, and beautiful bouquets of flowers as centrepieces. Everyone sat down; Brody beside Bella, Charlotte beside Zach, Lacy beside Thom, Allison beside Jim, Barb beside Tammy, and Jeff, Rob and Pete sat at the end of the table. The aroma in the air was making everybody hungry.

"Well, thanks for coming everybody. Allison and I are so happy to host a group of such lovely people. Thom, Charlotte, Bella, it's been such a pleasure to get to know all of you. We'll definitely miss you. Cheers everybody," Jim raised his drink as everyone else saluted and clinked their glasses.

As the cheers finished, Maggie began dropping off bowls of soup and dinner rolls to the table. Everyone was hungry and commenting on the smell of the soup.

"Now, before everyone digs in, this stew and broth is made from the bear we all encountered last night at 3am. Now you might think it's strange, but I wanted the bear to become part of us and share in the glory. You don't have to eat it, but you may be pleasantly surprised."

"This is delicious," Pete said.

"What's the cut of meat in here?" Thom asked.

"That's the tenderloin," Jim said.

Everyone tried the stew and were nodded in affirmation.

"Delicious, right?" Jim asked.

Bella and Charlotte looked at each other and shrugged their shoulders. "It's actually not that bad," Charlotte said as she took another spoonful.

"Well, now the bear is officially a part of me," Bella said, taking another spoonful.

"Can't say I've ever had bear before," Lacy said to Thom.

"First for me too," Thom replied laughing.

The stew was a hit, both as a delicious starter and metaphoric symbol of the hikers conquering nature the night before. Everyone finished their stew and Maggie cleared the dishes as everyone kept chatting. Zach and Charlotte secretly held hands underneath the table, while Brody helped put the necklace around Bella's neck.

An emboldened Pete stood and raised his glass. "Ladies and gentlemen. Everyone here is truly lucky to have Thom, Bella, and Charlotte in their lives. Even though they are leaving tomorrow, I know we will see them again. I just hope the next time we see Thom, he's gotten a little better at his short game." Everyone gave a little chuckle. "Though it's only been a couple weeks, it feels like we've known you for a long time. It's been nice getting to know you guys. Cheers everybody." Pete raised his glass even higher and sat back down as he clinked glasses with Jeff and Rob.

"Thanks, Pete. It means a lot," Thom said down the table. "I don't think you realize how important each one of you are. You've been fun, kind, generous, hospitable, funny, and gracious. I feel, and I'm pretty sure my daughters feel, like new people since we've been here. The mountains, the lakes, the adventures, have all transported us to such a great place, and for that we all thank you."

Everyone clapped at Thom's kind words and smiled back in his direction.

"Now, for the main course, we are not eating any more bear," Jim joked. "I've made a beautiful beef roast with potatoes and grilled asparagus. The roast is medium rare, and I hope this works for everybody. Anybody like their beef medium to well?" Jim looked around to find nobody protesting. "Wonderful." Jim turned toward Maggie and gave her a nod as she went back into the kitchen.

Allison rose to her feet and went back behind the bar to grab a couple bottles of red wine. She opened the 1993 Burgundies and poured everyone a glass, except for Charlotte, Bella, Zach, and Brody. Allison was a great host and had sommelier training. She loved wine and creating the lodge selection, year after year. "This is a 1993 Chateau de la Tour Burgundy. Beautiful wine, with blackberry and tobacco hints with an excellent finish," she said proudly.

"This is fantastic," Lacy said, sipping the vintage.

Maggie delivered the 13 plates of roast beef, potatoes, and asparagus and everyone began eating. Maggie returned to top up water glasses and check to see if anyone needed anything else and then made her way back behind the bar. The smell of garlic, rosemary, and oregano filled the dining room, as the supper was enjoyed by all.

Allison watched her son talking with Bella with such joy. Brody had dated girls, but the way he spoke to and listened to Bella was new to Allison. Brody maintained eye contact, showed support, and laughed like he did when he was just a boy. Though he was still young, he was acting like an adult. She thought about how well she and her husband had taught him.

Barb and Tammy were having a great time, as well. They watched their best friend, Lacy, falling in love with Thom. Both Tammy and Barb knew how smart, independent, and driven Lacy was and that it would take a special somebody to sway her heart. They noticed the love in Thom's eyes. Tammy nudged Barb. "I think they're in love."

"It seems legitimate," Barb whispered back.

"But he is leaving," Tammy said quietly.

"If it's meant to be, it's meant to be," Barb said. "I don't think they're going to let this go."

"I'll never let go, Jack," Tammy said pretending to sob, like Rose from Titanic.

Brody got up and helped Maggie clear the table without being asked. "Thanks, Brody," Maggie said.

"No problem," Brody said.

"Our boy is growing up," Allison whispered as she leaned into Jim.

"Taking initiative. Just like his mom," he said as they shared a kiss.

Maggie and Brody helped to bring out a colourful cake with the words 'We Will Miss You' written in icing. Maggie placed the cake in front of a smiling Thom, Bella, and Charlotte.

"We will all miss you," Jim said as Brody brought some small plates and dessert napkins.

"Thanks everyone. I certainly didn't have these expectations when I left Toronto. I mean, I didn't expect to meet so many people and become friends with them. Charlotte and Bella are also grateful they didn't have to hang out with just their Dad," Thom said as everyone snickered. "Banff is such a special place to me, and now to my daughters. Barb, Tammy, Lacy, thanks for taking my girls to the spa and being such great mentors. Jeff, Rob, Pete, thanks for the laughs and keeping things light; next time I see you, I'm gonna beat you at golf. Brody, Allison, Jim, you've been gracious hosts and I can't thank you enough for the five-star accommodations. And, oh yeah, a big thank you to Jim for keeping us alive last night."

Everyone chuckled as Maggie came by the table and filled up coffee for everyone. Allison cut and distributed the cake around the table as Lacy rose to her feet.

"Hi everyone," Lacy addressed the table. "I rarely hit on tourists, but Thom certainly changed my perspective. Thom, Charlotte, Bella, I'm so glad we got to know each other. Bella, whatever you choose, whichever school you decide to go to, I know you're going to excel and shine like the star you are." Bella smiled back at Lacy. "Charlotte, I've never met a teenager who has made me laugh as much as you have. Your charm, beauty and quirkiness will carry you far through life. And Thom, you're the cutest tourist I've ever met. Spending time with you has been one of the most joyful, exciting, death-defying experiences of my life. I'm looking forward to going on more adventures with you."

Thom couldn't help but feel a surge of melancholy overcome him, as he shed a tear. Flashes of hiking, reaching summits, swimming, sharing laughs, and the first time they met at the coffee shop passed through Thom's mind as Jim signalled to Maggie. Maggie pressed play on the CD player and 'We'll Meet Again' came on the stereo. Barb and Jeff got up and shared a dance, Tammy and Rob followed, then Allison and Jim, Charlotte and Zach, then Bella and Brody.

Pete was the lone person left at the end of the table. Maggie crept up behind him and tapped him on the shoulder. "Want to dance?"

Pete looked up. "That would be divine," he said as he got up and danced with the bartender.

The entire group, full and feeling merry, danced the night away.

Chapter 13 - The Return

The flight ascended from Calgary through the clouds as it headed east to Toronto. Bella stared out the window across the clouds and contemplated everything that had happened over the past few weeks. Charlotte was asleep almost instantly. Thom looked Charlotte's way and gave a little chuckle at her mouth being wide open. Thom went back to the book he was reading as the plane soared 30,000 feet above sea level.

Thom was having trouble concentrating on reading; he couldn't stop thinking about Lacy. He remembered his deal falling through and that he would need to connect with his real estate agent as soon as he got back. He also remembered how busy he was going to be with his engineering firm. Thom liked being busy and dedicated to his career, but a major part of him loved recreation. He loved hiking, exploring, climbing, fresh air, and camping. He promised himself that he would dedicate more of his time to being outdoors in Ontario. He slowly drifted off as the plane hummed him to sleep.

The plane landed at Pearson Airport around 6:00pm at night in the pouring rain. After Charlotte, Bella, and Thom picked up their luggage, they made their way outside to find their car that had been parked for 2 weeks. As soon as the doors opened to the outside, all three of them immediately felt the sluggish, hot, humid air. It was thick and smoggy with no hints of freshness. It was a rude welcome back to Toronto, Ontario.

"Lord almighty, is this what the weather is always like in Toronto?" Bella asked.

"We're not in the mountains anymore," Thom said as they crossed the street into the parking garage.

"My clothes are already sticking to me," Charlotte said as she plucked her shirt away from her body.

"I can't believe we've been breathing this air our whole lives. This is nothing like Alberta," Bella said.

"Pretty shocking, isn't it?" Thom replied.

"It's gross," Charlotte said as Thom validated the parking ticket he had kept in his wallet.

They made their way home in the rain and finally made it after suffering through the weather and the 401-highway traffic. Thom was especially glad to have made it home in one piece. Travelling was particularly exhausting, and he knew he and the girls would have to re-adjust to the time zones once again. They unloaded the car and made their way inside to a lonely, empty house.

To Charlotte and Bella, things immediately felt depressing and different. They realized the toxicity of the house. They immediately had flashbacks of their mom cooking in the kitchen and reading to them on the couch and gardening in the backyard. Both girls recognized that being reminded of their mother at every turn was not always good for the healing process. They felt they had taken gigantic strides in the healing process, only to have old feelings of nostalgia, hostility, and resentment return.

Bella went to her room immediately, dropped her luggage and lay down on her queen-sized bed. She looked at the ceiling and began to cry. It was a soothing cry, after such an emotional journey.

As she wiped and rubbed her eyes, she slowly drifted off, still wearing her shoes and clothes.

Charlotte did some laundry and made herself some crackers and peanut butter, about the only thing left to eat in the barren kitchen. She wanted to call her friends and tell them about her adventures, Zach, the bear, the views, but it was getting late, and she was getting drowsy.

Thom came into the kitchen and sat down across from Charlotte. "Hey pumpkin. Can I have one?" he asked.

"Sure," Charlotte said.

"You doing alright?" Thom asked.

"Yeah. A little sad, but hanging in there," Charlotte answered.

"I'm a little sad too. It always happens when I get back from vacation."

"When does it start to feel better?" Charlotte asked.

"I remember getting back from Florida, where it was 30 degrees and balmy and coming back to minus 17-degree weather in a snowstorm. Me and your mother were miserable. But we woke up the next morning, after a long sleep and felt a million times better."

"Yeah, that makes sense. I'm tired." Charlotte understood the logic of her Dad.

"I just turned on the A/C, so you'll sleep like a baby. Finish up your snack, brush your teeth, hop into bed and I'll see you in the morning," Thom said as he got up and turned to leave.

"Hey Dad."

"Yeah?" he said, spinning around.

"Thanks for the best vacation I've ever had. It was so much fun," Charlotte said with a smile.

"No problem, kiddo. There's no one else I would've wanted to spend it with." Thom turned and went upstairs to bed while Charlotte finished her snack, rinsed off her plate, and went upstairs.

Charlotte slipped into bed and reminisced about going to the Rose and Crown, having too much tequila, and puking in a garden bed. She chuckled to herself, closed her eyes and soon thereafter, fell sound asleep.

Thom washed his face, brushed his teeth, and got into bed with the intention of reading. It only took a couple of pages, before he fell asleep with the book laid across his chest.

The sun woke everyone at the house at around the same time. It was a still, sunny, hot morning in Toronto. The sound of streetcars, dogs, bikes, birds chirping and children at play could be heard throughout the streets. Bella looked out her window to see a team of five city workers cutting down a tree and chipping the branches into the back of a green truck. It was too early for heavy machinery, she thought to herself.

Bella came downstairs to her Dad who was wearing a nice dress shirt and khaki pants. Charlotte was still in her pyjamas eating a bowl of cereal.

"I went out and grabbed some milk and apples, if you want to have some cereal, Bella," Thom said as he sipped his morning coffee.

"Great. I'm starving," Bella responded. "Where are you off to?"

"I'm heading into work; gonna try and get on top of things," Thom said. "Remember about looking into schools. Deadline is next week for late acceptance. You'd better hurry and make a decision. I will support you and whatever you choose."

"Ok, I will," Bella said, unsure of herself.

"You have no idea, do you?" Charlotte said to Bella.

"Eat your cereal, peasant," Bella snapped back.

"Ok, I'm outta here," Thom said as he gathered his things. "I've left your transit passes on the table by the front door."

"Thanks Dad," Charlotte and Bella said at the same time.

Thom left out the front door, carrying a set of blueprints and his briefcase while Bella and Charlotte ate breakfast.

"Why does dad have so much energy today?" Charlotte asked.

"No clue."

"What are you doing today?"

"I'm going to check out the Ryerson campus downtown," Bella said. "What are you doing today?"

"I'm gonna head over to Keagan's place, I think we're going to High Park in the afternoon," Charlotte said.

Keagan was Charlotte's best friend and confidant. They were always at the same school, playing the same sports, and interested in the same boys. Keagan was one of the only friends Charlotte had kept in high school since her mother passed away.

"Tell Keagan I said hello," Bella said.

"No problem."

Thom had forgotten how busy this city was, especially the downtown commute. He was on an early subway train and stood shoulder to shoulder with thousands of people. After spending so long in the spacious Rocky Mountains, he realized he had a bit of a case of claustrophobia. He had started at the Royal York Subway and only made it a few stops to Runnymede until he had to get off.

As soon as he got off the train, he immediately felt better as he had room to breathe and stretch his legs. He walked east toward downtown; he passed High Park and through the Junction where Dundas crossed Bloor Street. Before long he started south on Bathurst and was downtown in no time. The walk seemed a blur to Thom who typically stopped to smell the roses. He had never experienced anything like claustrophobia before and yet now was aware of its existence.

Thom made his way into the high-rise where his firm was located, smiled, said 'hello' to the security guard, and made his way to the elevators. The first door opened and had several passengers. "I'll get the next one," he said as everyone looked at him with what seemed to be distain. The next elevator came, and the same thing happened. "I'll wait for the next one," Thom said as everyone stared stone-faced back in his direction. "Maybe I'll just wait for an empty elevator all day," he said to himself as a businesswoman shot him a dirty look.

Eventually he got onto an elevator with only a few people. His nerves were calming down, but he still felt the need to break the silence. "Hot one out there, eh?" Thom said casually.

"Yeah," one lady said.

"Yep," a man said.

Thom was upset at himself. This didn't seem right. His nerves were getting the best of him. Eventually he made it into his office on the 66th floor. He opened his door to find a stack of files and blueprint tubes. He didn't know where to start. He dropped his things, made his way to the staff lounge, and brewed a pot of coffee. He knew it wasn't a good idea, but he had to procrastinate somehow.

He sat down at his desk with a cup of coffee, let out a big exhale, and began the exhaustive process of sorting through and finalizing a few of the firm's projects.

Bella found herself having similar feelings to Thom when she was on the subway downtown, but it wasn't as extreme, and she was able to make it through the ride. The air was putrid downtown, especially on the subway platform, which smelled like urine and sweat. She was looking forward to getting above ground and seeing the sunshine. But she forgot that downtown, the sun was typically blocked by a building or two. The high-rises were daunting, the heat was staggering, and it seemed like there was no oxygen at street level.

Bella was a few blocks from the Dundas Subway station when she first set her eyes on the Ryerson campus. The school had just recently been granted university status and wanted the necessary funds to conduct research and establish graduate programs. Huge '50-year Anniversary' banners hung outside all the different buildings. She visited the architecture building, the school of interior design, the athletics centre, the campus store, and student centre. Nothing really impressed her. She noticed the abundance of grey around campus, the buildings, the benches, the lockers, the bike racks, the sidewalks; it all seemed very barren and gloomy. She hadn't noticed one green space on her tour or one place to sit outside and enjoy a lunch or study break. It was all very bleak. It did not excite her at all.

Charlotte and Keagan walked through High Park, through the trails and paths, past the zoo and the sports fields, and eventually took a seat at the pond at the south end of the park. The two best friends talked about Zach, the bear who wandered into their camp, the numerous hikes, the new people they met and the overall adventure of Alberta.

"I'm going to have to admit, I'm kind of jealous. It sounds like it was an awesome vacation," Keagan said.

"I want to go back so bad," Charlotte said. "You should see the mountains, Keagan. They're enormous, it's like having an art exhibit wherever you go."

"Screw the exhibit. I wanna meet Zach and his friends," Keagan joked.

"The punk show was awesome. It was a band called 'Stoner Haze,' because they were from a town called 'Stoner' in B.C.," Charlotte explained.

"Classic," Keagan said. "Were they any good?"

"They were awesome," Charlotte said, looking out on the pond.

The two friends were so happy to see each other, it seemed like they hadn't been together in an eternity. There was about a month and a half before school started and they were determined to have the best time in their senior year. They talked about playing volleyball, basketball, going to prom, walking across the stage at graduation, and saying goodbye to their adolescent years.

Keagan certainly helped to alleviate the pain of leaving the first boy Charlotte actually liked. She made Charlotte laugh and look forward to the future. For the past couple of years, after the death of Valerie, Keagan was steadfast in Charlotte's life, even though anyone of sound mind would have walked away from Charlotte and the demon she had become. Keagan put up with outbursts, the vileness, and the rudeness of Charlotte, and never said anything against her. Keagan knew in her heart that Charlotte was being torn apart and her role was to keep her together and moving forward.

Keagan recognized the difference in Charlotte right away. She certainly seemed more positive and optimistic, but she also was floored by her openness, honesty, and sincerity.

The two girls made their way back north to Bloor Street, through the park, and eventually back home. When they got back to Charlotte's house, she showed Keagan the necklace that Zach had bought for Charlotte and swooned at the thought of a sweet, thoughtful teenage boy. She showed Keagan the dream catcher she now hung on the wall above her bed.

"I bought you a gift too," Charlotte said to Keagan.

"You didn't have to do that."

"After everything you've done for me. Yes, I do," Charlotte insisted.

"What do you mean?" Keagan asked.

"You've put up with a lot of my crap. I just want to thank you for always being a good friend," Charlotte said sincerely.

Keagan opened the gift and revealed a red flannel shirt and leather belt with a gigantic bear-shaped belt buckle.

"This is fricking amazing, Char. Where did you find this?"

"In Banff; the Great Canadian Flannel Company. Let the belt remind you of the time me and Bella were almost eaten by a grizzly bear," Charlotte said.

"I still don't know if I believe you or not," Keagan jokingly said.

"Everyone in Alberta loves flannel, Keags. They eat in it, sleep in it, work in it, play in it," Charlotte joked.

As the girls joked and told stories, they heard the front door open. "Hello?" Thom said from the bottom of the stairs.

"Hey Dad! Is it okay if Keagan stays for dinner?" Charlotte yelled out her bedroom door.

"No problem!" he yelled back.

"Wanna play cribbage?" Charlotte asked.

"When did you learn how to play cribbage?" Keagan asked.

"My Dad's friend Lacy taught us all sorts of card games."

"Ok, teach me," Keagan said, clearly interested.

Thom began preparing dinner in the kitchen. He was chopping some veggies for a traditional marinara sauce when Bella came through the door looking rather miserable. "Hey," she unenthusiastically said to her Dad.

"Hi sweetie," Thom said, looking up. "What's the matter?"

"I don't know. Ryerson doesn't seem like a good fit," Bella said.

"Well, listen to your instincts. Go visit York and U of T tomorrow," Thom suggested.

"Yeah," Bella said as she went upstairs.

Thom thought to himself that it wasn't just a miserable day for him, but potentially for his daughter too. He put a pot of water to boil on the stove and pulled the spaghetti out of the cupboard. As he turned the stove on, the phone rang. Thom picked it up. "Hello?"

"Hi Mr. Hudson. It's Brody, how are you, sir?"

"Doing great, Brody."

"How was your flight? I'm glad you made it home alright," Brody said.

"It was great. We're all still in one piece," Thom said. "I'll get Bella for ya." Thom covered the phone. "Bella! Telephone!" he yelled up the stairs.

"Hello?" Bella picked up the phone in her room and Thom hung up his end.

"Bella, it's Brody."

"Hey Brody. It's so good to hear your voice," Bella said.

"I'm just on a little break at the lodge. What are you doing?" Brody asked.

"I went down to Ryerson today and checked out the campus."

"How was it? Did you like it?" Brody inquired.

"It is very urban. Lots of grey buildings; felt like the old Soviet Union. Not a lot of green space. No mountains, no glacial lakes, no hot springs; it's lame," Bella answered. "What are you up to?"

"Just working. Me and some friends are heading to Jasper on the weekend. I wish you could come with us."

"Me too," Bella said with a frown.

"So how was the flight back?" Brody asked.

"It was okay. We had lukewarm chicken parmesan and watched 'The Wedding Singer'. That was a funny movie. Have you seen it?" Bella asked.

"Yeah, it was classic. Sandler cracks me up. I actually liked the song he sings on the plane in the end," Brody said.

"Same."

"So, when are you coming back out west?" Brody said laughing as he shifted the conversation.

"Geez, I don't know," Bella said.

"I'm just kidding, but I miss you already. Hey, I have to get going, but could I call you later on?" Brody asked.

"Yeah sure. We're just about to sit down for dinner. Call me anytime," Bella answered.

"Great. Nice to hear your voice. Talk to you later."

"Bye."

"Bye bye," Brody said.

Bella hung up the phone and sprawled out on her bed and rumbled her lips as she exhaled. Charlotte barged into Bella's room.

"Who was that?" Charlotte drilled.

"It was Brody. He was just on a short break at the lodge," Bella answered.

"Cool. What's he up to?" Charlotte drilled again.

"I don't know. Tossing salad? Stirring soup? Setting tables?" Bella joked.

"Girls! Supper time!" Thom yelled from the bottom of the stairs.

Bella, Charlotte, and Keagan went downstairs and sat at the dining room table which was set with plates, forks, knives, and spoons. Thom brought in a big pot of spaghetti and another dish of marinara and meatballs.

"Smells good dad," Charlotte said.

"Certainly does," Keagan added.

"Hi Keagan. How are you?" Thom asked as he sat down. "It's been a while."

"I'm doing well," Keagan answered.

"I'm sure you've heard all about the excitement out west," Thom said.

"Sounded like a fun time. I don't think Charlotte wanted to leave," Keagan said as she turned and looked at Charlotte.

"I don't think any of us wanted to leave," Thom said as he looked at both Bella and Charlotte.

"I heard Crocodile Dundee had to shoot a bear, then you ate it," Keagan said.

"Yes, Crocodile Dundee did save our life," Thom said with a smile.

The four of them ate spaghetti and meatballs and talked about the various adventures throughout the vacation and how alien Banff seemed to the lifestyle of Torontonians. Thom truly reflected on the moods and attitudes of both him and his daughters as the sun set on the midsummer's night.

A week passed and things didn't seem to be getting any better. Despite keeping contact with Lacy and speaking on the phone with her almost every night, Thom felt more depressed as each day passed. Moving from subway to elevator, streetcar to store, one box to the next, he was truly feeling the meaning of the rat race. He hadn't seen a sunrise, a sunset, stars, or any other type of natural landscape to make him feel at ease since he returned.

He tried to make an effort to plan a day trip with the girls to a provincial park but plans kept falling through. Bella and Charlotte's enthusiasm for the outdoors was diminishing as quickly as his. Work was busy, which didn't help the situation. The firm had hard deadlines and commitments that put Thom under pressure. He was spending extra hours at the office and away from his daughters.

Throughout the week, Bella had visited all the university campuses she had applied to and soon realized none of them excited her. She felt a strong connection to the mountains, the energy, the air, and sense of belonging.

Charlotte was falling back into passive-aggressive behaviour. She was becoming rude, selfish, and stubborn as the days passed without a healthy lifestyle. Thom paid close attention to the sudden change. Lacy had suggested creating a weekly planner of activities to help her focus and reconnect with nature, but to no avail. Charlotte was desperately searching for independence and responsibility but was going about it all wrong. Thom suggested getting a part-time job, which she adamantly declined due to all her high school commitments. Thom was at a crossroads.

Chapter 14 - The Crossroads

Thom sat in his office around 6:00pm after a hard day at work. Though he seemed to have been productive, the work kept piling up even after weeks back at his desk. He wanted to take control of his life. He kept hearing from family and friends that running your own business was not only rewarding, but incredibly freeing and enlightening. He knew architecture, he knew construction, and he understood the basics of contracting. He asked himself if he could ever start a business and become his own boss.

He called his real estate agent and talked about new homes, selling his home and the housing market in general. He then called his parents who lived hours away in North Bay, Ontario. He talked to them about the vacation and asked them both for advice about his and the girl's future. He called his accountant to figure out his finances, then he called the girls at home to let them know he would be running late. Then he got up the nerve to call Lacy.

Bella and Charlotte laid on the couch watching television and flipping through magazines. They both seemed distant from one another as Thom came in through the front door.

"Hey girls. I brought a pizza," Thom said.

"I'm not hungry," Charlotte snapped.

"Neither am I," Bella added.

"Suit yourself," Thom said.

"Dad, we need to talk," Bella said seriously.

"Ok, I've got a few things to run by you too," Thom said as he dropped his briefcase and sat down on the couch.

"Dad don't get upset," Bella started.

"Well, I don't like where this is going," Thom said.

"Don't worry. I've talked to Brody, Allison, and Jim and I think I'm going to take a gap year and work in Banff. They said they can give me work and help me find a place to live. They know a couple of people who own rental properties."

"What about school?" Thom asked.

"I'm going to look into the University of Calgary and the University of Alberta," Bella said. "They've got some incredible programs, but I'm not sure exactly what I want to do right now."

"Well, that seems fair and honest. No sense in rushing into anything if you're not sure what you want to do," Thom said.

"What do you think?" Bella asked.

"I think that's a great idea," Thom said with a smile. "It takes some great maturity to listen to your instincts."

"You do?" Bella said, surprised by his response.

Thom turned to Charlotte. "What do you think?"

"I don't know. Kind of jealous, I guess," Charlotte said.

"I've been doing some thinking too. I want your opinion on this. I was thinking about starting my own contracting business, selling the house, and moving to Banff."

"Are we all thinking the same thing?" Bella said.

"I wasn't," Charlotte interjected.

"We wouldn't go anywhere until we sold the house and found a suitable place," Thom said.

"This is my final year of high school," Charlotte pleaded. "You want me to leave in my last year?"

"No, no," Thom said. "I've spoken with Keagan's parents, and they would be happy if you stayed with them in your final months at E.C.I. They have a big extra room they agreed to rent to me, under a few conditions."

"Does Keagan know this?" Charlotte asked.

"No, not until we discuss it, then you can talk to Keagan about it," Thom said as he glanced at Bella then back to Charlotte. "I know this is sudden, but I think it's going to be great."

"So, you're not coming to my volleyball games, no prom pictures, or coming to my graduation?" Charlotte teared up.

"Sweetie, I'll be there for your graduation, I'll take your picture at prom. I'll fly you and Keagan out to Alberta for March break. We can spend the Christmas holidays up at Grandma and Grandpa's. I promise the year will fly by. You'll have to do some dishes, do your own laundry, and cook the occasional meal, but nothing you can't handle. Then once the year is over, you can do whatever you want. You can stay in Ontario, you could come out to Alberta, heck you could go to Australia if you wanted, whatever you need."

"It kind of seems like it could be fun," Charlotte said. "It's only nine months. Me and Keagan might hate each other by the end, but I'm sure we would get over it."

"I'm so glad to be having this conversation with you girls. I didn't think a vacation to Alberta would be such a glaring wake-up call," Thom said with a relieved voice.

"Dad, I hate the schools around here. I feel like I belong in the mountains," Bella said.

"Your mom felt the same way, kiddo," Thom said.

"As soon as I got back here, I felt depressed. I don't think that's healthy," Bella followed up.

"I'm gonna get straight A's, win a city championship, go to prom, graduate, then come out west and bug the crap out you guys," Charlotte joked as all three shared a laugh.

"I'm going to put in my two-weeks-notice tomorrow at work," Thom said with a smile. "My real estate agent says the market is hot right now, so we're going to put the house on the market right away and I'm selling the car and buying a truck and trailer."

"Does Lacy know all this is happening?" Bella asked.

"Yes, she does. She told me to start the business, buy the truck, and move out west," Thom said. "She even invited us to stay with her at her house."

There was a long pause. Charlotte was clearly thinking deeply. "What if I did my last year of high school in Banff?" she asked.

"It certainly is an option, but I thought you would want to stay here with all your friends, play volleyball and do the whole prom/grad thing."

"Keagan's the only person I would miss. Plus, I'm sure I could play volleyball out there."

Thom smiled with pride at his youngest daughter. "It's up to you, button. We might have to transfer your Ontario credits, but I don't think it will be a problem. I could call the school board tomorrow."

"You should come out west, Char," Bella said.

Charlotte welled up in tears. She looked at her sister and Dad. Visions of her Mom nodding in agreement came into her head as she cried and jumped and hugged both her Dad and Bella.

"I wanna go with you!" Charlotte exclaimed.

Thom handed in his letter of resignation the next day and amicably worked the next two weeks to secure his professional reference. His company and boss were truly sad to see him go. The last day he cleaned out his office, including the picture of Val, Charlotte, Bella, and himself at Niagara Falls. It was a good run downtown for Thom, as he turned off the lights and said his 'goodbyes' to everyone. He took his last elevator ride down to the lobby with a giant grin on his face.

Charlotte transferred her Ontario academic credentials over to Alberta and was now officially a Banff Bear. Bella was going to start a job as a waitress at Jim and Allison's lodge and Thom had secured his first residential building contract already, via Jeff's friend in Canmore. Things were moving fast for everyone.

The Toronto house sold over-asking price as soon as it hit the market, much to the relief of Thom. His real estate agent came to the house and slapped the sold sticker on the real estate sign with Thom. The next day Charlotte, Bella, and Thom had a massive estate sale, each making money selling every little knick-knack in the house. They sold the living room furniture, some appliances, lamps, dressers, pictures, old toys, and even the beds. It was incredibly gratifying for Thom and the girls, but emotional at the same time, as they had to let go of all sorts of nostalgia.

Thom also purchased a large Chevy Silverado with a covered trailer that stored everything they were taking with them. That evening they ate pizza on the empty floor of the house, played board games and cards, and slept on air mattresses. It was a fun night as all three were anticipating the road trip across the country.

They had snacks, books, music, and games. This would be the first time any of them had driven across the country. The anticipation was tangible. They talked about where they wanted to stop and places they wanted to visit and marked them on the map.

Thom was incredibly delighted things had gone so smoothly that summer; the girls were happy, the house sold, he established his new business 'Bear Construction and Engineering' and was about to reconnect with Lacy, whom he couldn't stop thinking about.

The next morning, with the truck loaded and the house cleared, Thom left a note that read: *Wishing you a lifetime of great memories in your new home. Sincerely, the Hudsons.* He put the keys on top of the note and said goodbye to the house of a million memories. Visions of Valerie holding baby Bella, Charlotte swinging in the backyard, and the whole family playing board games flashed through his mind. He envisioned Valerie on the front porch as he shut the front door and walked down the steps. She waved to him and smiled. He couldn't help but smile as he got in the truck.

"What are you smiling at?" Charlotte asked.

"Nothing. I feel lucky, is all. Just thinking about your Mom and saying goodbye," Thom said.

Bella and Charlotte looked out the window and waved goodbye to their childhood home. Thom put his new truck in gear, and they pulled away down the road.

Chapter 15 - New Horizons

Thom, Bella, and Charlotte stopped for the night in Wawa, Ontario after being on the road for around ten hours. Long, winding highways carried them through the great Ontario forests until they reached the small lakeside town. The three of them got out and stretched their weary legs and made their way into the motel reception.

"Hi there, friends. I'm Ruth. How has the drive been so far? Are you looking for a room for the night?"

"Thanks Ruth. So far, so good. Yeah, a room with two double beds would be great," Thom said.

"Well, we do have a room with two queen sized beds," she said.

"That will be fine," Thom said as he handed her his credit card.

"Have you ever been to Wawa, girls?" Ruth asked Bella and Charlotte.

"No," Bella said.

"Nope," Charlotte followed.

"Well, have you ever heard of Winnie the Pooh?" Ruth asked.

"Yeah," Bella said as she noticed a framed poster of Winnie the Pooh with the phrase 'How lucky am I to have something that makes saying goodbye so hard' – A.A. Milne.

"Well, Winnie is a little black bear from these woods, just near Blind River up the road. A soldier and veterinarian named Harry Colebourn bought the little cub from a local trapper for $20 on his way over to Europe to fight in the Great War. Little Winnie got her name from Winnipeg where Colebourn was living. Winnie grew up as the regiment mascot and was loved by all. Colebourn donated Winnie to the London Zoo and that's when the author A.A. Milne and his son Christopher Robin visited her for the first time. The rest is history," Ruth said with a smile.

"Winnie the Pooh is from Wawa?" Thom asked in a surprised voice. "That's pretty special."

"You betcha," Ruth said proudly.

"First of all, I didn't know Winnie was an actual bear, and second of all, I did not know she was Canadian," Bella said.

"I didn't know she was named after Winnipeg," Charlotte said with a puzzled look on her face.

"Thanks Ruth. This has been an incredibly educational motel check-in," Thom said. "Bears seem to have brought us a lot of great luck this year."

"We are proud of Winnie around here. We serve breakfast at 7:00am, Mr. Hudson," Ruth said as she handed him keys. "Room 115. Straight down on the left."

"Thanks, Ruth. We'll see you in the morning," Thom said as he and the girls walked out the door.

Bella took a long, last look at the Winnie the Pooh poster and realized how lucky she was to say goodbye.

The next morning, after a big Wawa breakfast, they hit the road along the north shore of Lake Superior. They couldn't help but be in awe of the crystal-clear waters, the rocky bluffs and the sun that shone through the clouds to the bottom of the great lake. They could see schools of fish, fallen timbers, and rocks carved through thousands of years of deglaciation. Charlotte snapped a couple of pictures on her Pentax camera.

They stopped in Thunder Bay for lunch and gas and by nightfall they arrived in Winnipeg, where they stopped at a motel on the outskirts of town. They had spent 13 hours driving and were totally wiped. All three of them fell asleep almost immediately and it was morning in no time.

The next day, Thom, Bella, and Charlotte were exposed to the great Canadian Prairies; miles of endless grassland as they pushed on through Manitoba and into Saskatchewan.

"Do you know why nobody breaks up in Saskatchewan?" Thom asked the girls.

"Why?" Charlotte answered.

"Because you have to watch your ex walk away for two days."

"Funny," Bella said as Charlotte laughed.

The three pressed on along Highway #1 into Alberta. They would stay in Medicine Hat that night and arrive in Banff the next day. They knew they were getting close to Calgary and Banff. Bella called Brody from the Medicine Hat hotel and Thom called Lacy to let them know they would be arriving sometime in the afternoon.

The sunset on the prairie was a magical sight. Thom and the girls admired the curvature of the earth as the sky lit up with pinks, reds, and deep burgundy.

"Pretty, isn't it?" Thom said admiring the sky.

"Sure is," Bella said.

"Pretty special," Charlotte said as she snapped another photo. "Let's take one together."

Charlotte handed her Dad the camera, he wound the film, held the camera out as far as he could and squished them all together and snapped the photo. "Awkward self-photos are the worst," he said, handing back the camera to Charlotte.

The morning sunrise was just as beautiful as the sunset the night before. Thom had awoken early, made his way across the street and got tea and coffee for himself and the girls. When he got back to the room, the girls were stirring.

"I brought you some tea, girls," Thom said. "By this afternoon we'll be in the Rocky Mountains."

"Thanks," Bella moaned.

"Thanks, Dad," Charlotte added.

"Jump in the shower and we'll hit the road by 9am. Sound good?" Thom asked.

"Sounds good," Charlotte said.

"10-4," Bella added.

Both girls were both excited for their new beginning in Alberta. The drive from Medicine Hat gave them their first experience of the rolling hills and cattle fields of the province. Once they made their way into Calgary, things became a lot more familiar. Bella was certainly interested in the University of Calgary as they passed by. Charlotte pointed out the Calgary Tower as they passed and reminisced from earlier in the summer. The Rocky Mountains started as they made their way past Calgary and through the tiny foothills. Both Thom and the girls had the feeling they were going home. They passed Canmore and took the exit to Banff. The truck and trailer drove through the streets that inspired all three of them so much.

Thom pulled the truck over in front of Lacy's House. He ran up to the house and found a note on the door. It read: *Thom, Bella, and Charlotte. Hi, I'm at the Rose and Crown for lunch with a client. Walk down and meet me.* Thom went back to the truck and told the girls they were going to walk down to the Rose and Crown for a bite to eat and meet Lacy. All three were happy to stretch their legs. As soon as Bella and Charlotte stepped out of the truck, they noticed the air quality right away.

"You smell that?" Charlotte asked.

"What?" Bella said.

"No stink," Charlotte said.

"Okay, are you ready for a little walk after three days in a truck?" Thom asked.

"Hell yes!" Charlotte screamed.

"Damn straight," Bella added.

They headed down the street and passed Lacy's neighbour Bob walking his dog, Hank.

"Howdy neighbour," Bob said, and Hank gave a little bark.

"Hey, how are you?" Thom replied.

"Days like this, how could I ever complain?" Bob said with a smile.

Charlotte and Bella gave the retriever a scratch behind the ears, and they went their separate ways.

"I think you should get a dog, Dad," Charlotte said.

"Maybe someday," Thom answered with a smug smile.

Eventually they arrived at the Rose and Crown and made their way upstairs to the establishment. As soon as they entered the room, they saw Lacy, Jim, Allison, Brody, Zach, Tammy, Barb, Jeff, Rob, Pete, and Maggie.

"Surprise!" everyone shouted.

Thom, Bella, and Charlotte were shocked to see the gathering of people. So many bright smiles. Bella ran and jumped into the arms of Brody. Charlotte ran and hugged Zach. Thom and Lacy hugged and kissed as if they hadn't seen each other in years. Everyone was so happy to see one another.

Though it had only been a couple of months, it seemed longer to Bella, Charlotte, and Thom. They had gone through a rollercoaster of a summer. High highs and low lows. Thom had quit

234

a job, sold his house and car, Bella had switched her post-secondary thinking completely, and Charlotte was finishing her diploma in a completely different school.

It had certainly been a summer to never forget. It started as a vacation to the mountains and morphed into a permanent relocation to a national park. Thom, Bella, and Charlotte knew it was the best decision they ever made.

Jim handed Thom a large, wrapped gift. Thom promptly tore it apart to reveal a large grizzly bear skin.

"Welcome back, Thom," Jim said. "That is what you think it is."

Thom looked up to Jim, smiled and shed a tear of joy as Charlotte and Bella leaned in and hugged their dad.

The End.

Manufactured by Amazon.ca
Acheson, AB